The Incredible Double

Owen Hill

The Incredible Double
By Owen Hill

ISBN: 978-1-60486-083-2
LCCN: 2009901377

PM Press
PO Box 23912
Oakland, CA 94623
www.pmpress.org

Layout: Karl Kersplebedeb
Cover: John Yates

Printed in the USA, on recycled paper.

Lines from Edward Dorn's *Gunslinger and Abhorrences* are
quoted with permission. Thanks to Jennifer Dorn.

Thanks also to those who read and listened to
passages of this novel before publication.

this book is for Liz Leger

a cultural patchwork fit for a fool
in the only country in the world
with a shop called the Drug Store

— Edward Dorn, *Abhorrences*

1.

My '87 Tercel is in great shape, only a hundred thousand miles and new almost everything, but it does have trouble with the Bay Area hills. Coming out of the tunnel on 24, leaving Berkeley, heading toward the suburbs, I was losing speed and the SUVs were losing patience. I shifted it down into second and wagged my middle finger. My best friend Marvin says that driving slow in a small car is a revolutionary act. Maybe he's right. A woman in a Hummer, no lie, who probably weighed in at 97 pounds, half of it hair, gave me a look that could kill and, waved her phone at me. When you think of spoiled little brats in military vehicles careening through the 'burbs, you know how rotten the twenty-first century will be.

First insult that came out of my mouth was, "Gas eating pig!" Way too soft, lame, actually. I floored the Tercel, and through some miracle, I caught up. I had a half-drunk can of Mr. Pibb in my nifty little cup holder, the only extra on a stripped-down car. I grabbed the can, tossed it at the Hummer. Got more on it than one would expect. Testosterone? In a perfect world I would have sped up and left her in the dust. Not enough horsepower for that so I let off the gas and dropped back, soon to be passed by Rangers, Rams, Escolante... sweet revenge.

Tercels aren't equipped with Onstar so I unfolded the map, doing about 50 in the right-hand lane. More honks. Next time out this way, a six pack of Mr. Pibb. Two off-ramps later I was in beautiful Snorinda. Six-bedroom houses, big lawns. Ghetto for the overtaxed middle class. I pulled over and looked at the directions. 233 Merwin Place. A few quick turns and I was there. Big house with a tract-home look. Nothing special. Lots of parking out front. I like that. I made a mental note to get rich and move out of South Berkeley. Maybe next year.

The house was on a slight hill, not enough to make it look stately. Still, I'd never lived this well. The landscaping was hometown America, a carpet-length lawn and some well-trimmed bushes. Old Glory waved proudly, the pole bolted to what looked like a detached garage. I walked up the sloped driveway to the front door. Gave the doorbell a nice long press, didn't hear anything. Knocked. A Haystack Calhoun type answered the door. He was even wearing overalls. This didn't seem right.

"Are you Jerome Wally?"

"I'm a member of the staff. What can I do for you?" The lug spoke with a proper Brit accent. A walking mixed metaphor.

"Somebody named Jerome Wally asked me to come out. Said he couldn't come to me. I'm Clay Blackburn."

"Yes. The detective."

I nodded. I barely qualify. I don't have a license, don't carry a gun. I'm a book scout. But sometimes I take these jobs.

He took me through a cream-colored living room, all light and airy, that middle-class beige look. Sexy, in a twisted way. Fantasies of coming on the couch, making a mess.

We went through a yuppie-style kitchen, lots of hanging pots that didn't look used. Then through a backdoor to a well-trimmed little courtyard. A few feet back, there was large, square building that looked like a Motel 6. I was surprised that it couldn't be seen from the street. Hidden by trees and the front house, I guess. Jeeves/Jethro unlocked the ugly red door and let me in. To the left was a large room with a conference table. Parquet floors, a huge Franz Kline to die for, and an open staircase. I was lead up the stairs to a large, open, office/living space. My eyes were drawn to the Dean Martin era wetbar. I was getting the picture. Somebody was worth a bundle.

He came down another open staircase. He didn't look like Dino. He looked like Ross Perot, but with hair. Hair for the ages! Soap opera hair, silver and sprayed. Made Bill Clinton's hair look flat. Perhaps he was a TV preacher.

He crossed the room and gave me a Win Friends Influence People smile. Smarmy as all hell. A microsecond handshake, like he didn't want to touch me, and I thought, Likewise, I'm sure.

"So this is the detective! Such exciting work! I'm Jerry. So good of you to come."

"Actually I'm not a licensed detective. You should know that up-front."

"We know all of that. We do our research here." He motioned me to the couch. Thoughts of making an orgasm mess left my brain like the Japanese fled Godzilla. He sat down and crossed his legs in a way that was rather limp-wristed. I hoped he was gay and not bi. Didn't want to count him among my kind.

"Do you know who I am, Mr. Blackburn?"

I'd done a little research, too. "You're Jerry Wally, founder of Jerry's Drugs and More."

Another smarmy smile. "You must be wondering why I'm here."

Among other things, I thought. "You're based in Oklahoma, aren't you?"

"My home state, yes. But with hundreds of stores around the globe, I've become a citizen of the world. I'm based here for now because we've finally cracked the Bay Area market. We're opening fourteen stores in the coming months."

Except in Berkeley, where the city council gave him the bum's rush. Decided not to mention that. Just nodded and smiled. The old shuck and jive.

"I'll be doing some speaking engagements, overseeing construction, things like that. I was planning on staying in San Francisco, out by the Marina, but I was told by my security staff that this place would be safer." He gave the room a sour look. Low-class digs.

"What can I do for you?" I was getting antsy and wanted to cut to the chase.

"Apparently this place isn't completely safe. My whereabouts aren't as secret as we thought. I've been getting threats."

"Why not move?"

"Well, let me tell you, Mr. Blackburn. I don't like being bullied. I didn't build a financial empire by letting people push me around. Bad enough that Berkeley shut us out. Of course, that's temporary but it still stings. We have hundreds of stores the world over. We keep prices low. We do things right. Drugs and More stores provide a center, a public meeting place for the communities that they serve."

I had to shut him up, or hit him. Decided instead to cover my ears and sing. "Which Side Are You On," the first song that came to mind. Clay Blackburn fights absurdity with absurdity.

It didn't work. The fucker sang along with me.

"Bravo. Yes. The rights of the workers are my concern, too! That's why we pay a full dollar over the minimum wage. We're like a big family…"

"What do you want from me?"

"I'm getting death threats. Somebody in Berkeley."

"You have a security staff. You could also call the police, if you haven't already."

"I'm going to level with you Clay, because we're both men of the world. The police are useless in these cases. Not that I don't admire, no, revere them, for doing their all to keep America safe. But they are, between us, rather clunky. And as for my own staff, they're good. Really good. Gleaned from the Special Forces, mostly. They beat communism, these men. They captured Saddam, for heaven's sake! But Berkeley isn't Iraq. Berkeley is, well, really foreign to them. I had one of them, ex-CIA, I swear, tell me that Berkeley gives 'behind enemy lines' new meaning."

I sat up straight. Civic pride is a beautiful thing. "How do you know this person's from Berkeley?"

"Person. Not guy, person. So Berkeley. So quaint. Have I told you how much trouble we had opening a store in Madison? Had to Clarence Thomas 'em. Got a Black politician to take up the cause. But more of that later. The letters are postmarked Berkeley, and he signs himself T'Graph T. We figure he's some local nut. With all due respect, Clay, it takes one to know one. You could run him down and we'd be done with him."

Normally I'd get up and leave at this point. But a hungry wolf was camping on my doorstep. Book scouting was at its lowest point, what with Amazon selling used books for two cents plus postage. Only a couple of the big used bookstores could compete, and the competition to sell to them was furious. I was barely making rent.

"What's your fee, Clay?"

I work on a sliding scale. In my mind, I slid the scale as high as it would go. "My regular fee is $750 a day plus expenses, and another $500 a day when I employ my partner."

"I'll make it a straight $1,200 a day and you can use

him as you like. Or, as the natives say, use this person as you like."

A fair amount of scratch. If I could stay on the payroll for a month, I could spend serious time on the beach in Baja. I rarely have to address the issue of selling out, since, as the poet said, nobody is buying. Poetry, used books, low-rent detecting… a recipe for a life of near poverty. Marvin, my own personal Jiminy Cricket, would be pissed. He's an unrepentant Communist. But it's easier for him. He owns his house. I was conflicted, but it didn't feel so bad. I was, as they say, born in the USA, where money is love. I was flattered that somebody cared to the tune of $1,200 clams a day.

"Okay, Wally…"

"Jerry. Please call me Jerry."

"Here's how I work. I'll take a thousand up front. I'll poke around for a couple of days and see what I can see. If I can't do anything for you, that's that. If I think I can, the time clock starts ticking."

"Splendid. I'll write the check myself." As if that was some kind of favor.

2.

Jerry Wally had to rush off to a meeting, but one of his minions explained that there had been repeated short calls to Wally's cell, a number that only a few were supposed to be privy to. Two words, raspy voice. Kill you.

This being Sunday, I stayed in Snorinda and headed to a yard sale that I'd seen advertised on Craigslist. It was a very nice yard fronting a very nice house on a street that was, well, nice. The books didn't really fit the house, or the owners, who were so bland and forgettable that I'd be hard put to pick them out of a line-up. And me a detective.

Somebody there liked movie star books. I rescued a hardback copy of *Miss Tallulah Bankhead*, a great old Hollywood bio with lots of gossip column appeal. I knew I'd never be able to sell the thing, but I needed something to read anyway and it was in perfect condition. Had a vague thought that I would write a sequence of poems based on the life of that famous bisexual tippler.

I crossed the lawn with my new find, threw it into the backseat of the very warm Tercel. September is the best month in the Bay Area. Almost too warm (for once), and in Berkeley the new students are on parade, practically sans clothes. They get younger every year but that doesn't bother me. After all, Mohammed married a nine-year-old girl. I seem to lust after anything over seventeen. I'm almost above board.

Highway 24 was light of traffic, and soon I was parking next to People's Park, then walking down Dwight to The Chandler Apartments, semi-subtly ogling the youngsters as they walked to class. The old lobby was cool and dark. I took the stairs for the sake of exercise, up to the fourth floor where my cat Emily was waiting. Turned on the fans and got myself a Bohemia beer. Put on an old Violent Femmes CD and left a message at Marvin's. I needed his input on this new job. Knew what he'd say, but I wanted to hear him say it.

I walked down to Andronico's. It's overpriced but close to home. Walking up Telegraph Avenue I encountered Bruce, my favorite street nomad. He was sitting, kind of lopsided, propped up against the wall of the Eclair Bakery.

"Hi, Bruce. Kind of in a hurry."

Bruce rubbed his shaved head. He has a permanent knot, right side. Looks like a horn. "I have a sad story that I'll tell later. Do you have ten dollars?"

I gave him a dollar and rushed along.

Scouting hasn't been paying off in steaks lately, but now I could afford to splurge. Picked out a large, well-marbled New York, salad makings, and a loaf of Acme bread. Not very Berkeley of me, Marvin would say. But he'd love the steak.

3.

And he did. I had two bottles of Rombaur Cabernet left over from better times. Opened them both. No cocktails tonight. River of red wine. And then some port. Marvin barely spoke at first, savoring the wine and the meat. He was, as usual, wearing sweats and sweatshirt. Today it was a Moe's Books hoodie. His hair was limp and medium long. Was he trying to look like Neil Young? Why would anybody do that, I thought. But I didn't mention it. Hadn't brought up his appearance in all the years I'd known him.

"God, I love cow."

"Welcome to the food chain."

"Been there awhile. Not going to leave."

He poured himself a glass of the Rombaur, swirled and smelled. Strong look of approval.

I put the steaks on the stovetop grill for a few short minutes. Tossed the salad, removed the oven fries. Easiest meal on earth, unless you screw it up. This time it was perfect.

"Ever heard of Jerome Wally?"

"The rich guy?"

"Have you been in one of his stores?"

"A couple. You can't avoid them in America." To Marvin, anything east of Oakland and west of New York was America, another country. "I was doing some work in Oklahoma and I needed some stuff. They have those lunch counters, real retro. Good grilled cheese, though."

"He thinks somebody's trying to kill him. He wants me to do some snitching."

"He called you? Why? He must have a huge security force."

"Wants me to scope out the local color. His guys are too obvious."

"And you can walk the mean streets, the dive bars, the opium dens, the underbelly of south Berkeley."

"Something like that."

"The guy's a pig. Undercuts the competition, beats the unions. Middle America loves him, though. He's been born again, and he gives 'em cheap Twinkies."

"I've read the articles."

"I'm rooting for the killer."

"I thought you would. But I need the bucks. And I'm not normally pro-murder."

Marvin does something with computers that makes money. That's all I know. He's also an old lefty, and very active. After a few Negronis he's usually good for a story involving torching a cop car or destroying a hummer. I'm not sure how deep he's in, but if there's an underground out there he's heard of it. I asked him to get me some info and he rolled his eyes, shook his head. He wasn't going to help me protect this guy.

"C'mon, Marvin. I'm not asking you to vote Republican. I just want some background."

"Okay I'll get you some info on the capitalist, but I'm not going to help you snitch. That guy deserves to have the shit scared out of him."

I accepted that and went deep into the kitchen cabinet. Pulled out a nice bottle of cognac. Marvin beamed, and I changed the subject.

4.

Thanks to Mr. Drugstore, I could afford to coast. I had been living, barely, off of Ted Berrigan. Years before, I had bought a run of Berrigan books from the ex-boyfriend of a poet. She had left him flat to live in Spain with another poet who, I swear, went by the name of Sappho. The books had flowery inscriptions, like, "To Lucy in the Grand Piano... you are beautiful... take off that shirt!" The books occupied a sacred space on my shelf for a time, but at bottom I'm an unsentimental moneygrubber, as are all book scouts. When things got tough, I sold the books to Jeff Maser, a rare book dealer in West Berkeley, for a good price. Before buying them, he raised an eyebrow, said, "Are you sure these aren't Bob Dark forgeries?" A reference to a famous dirty dealer in the trade. I assured him that they were real, though I wasn't sure myself. Jeff nodded, thought about it, paid off in cash.

The Berrigan fund was nearly depleted when I got my detective's advance. And so it was that I strolled into Cesar's with no debt, a fistful of dollars, money in the bank. It was going to be a liquid summer. Bring on the dancing girls! Boys, too, for that matter.

I was wearing my favorite pair of black jeans and an SPD t-shirt. The sleeves were pretty short, just enough to show the bottom of my tattoo, a bright orange sun surrounded by the words of Giuseppe Ungaretti: ENORMITY ILLUMINES ME. I'm looking ten years younger than my age, I thought. It's like that when you're bucks up.

There were three open stools, a rarity at Cesar's. The tables were full. The tapas crowd was eating small food, possibly in anticipation of dinner at Chez Panisse next door. Berkeley-ites love to eat. Their love of food rivals the Italians. I took the middle stool and ordered a Negroni from my favorite bartender, a French guy with a shaved head. He iced the glass, mixed and shook with just the right dose of panache. I sipped and tasted, as I always do, savoring the ingredients: gin, Campari, a little vermouth. Perfect. The second sip was closer to a gulp. Heaven. I ordered some high-end fries, pulled the Bankhead biography out of my book bag. Life was good.

I was reading about a meeting with Libby Holman in a Rolls equipped with a Victrola and Bing Crosby records, thinking, I just wasn't made for these times, when I noticed her out of the corner of my eye, the way you do in bars. Dark hair with a hint of henna, scent of cigarettes and perfume. That's a rare scent in Berkeley. I was intrigued, but I didn't look at first. Waited for her to order. The voice got me. Almost too deep, and smoky. A drag queen? Oh well, wouldn't be the first time. But that's another story. She ordered Oban, rocks. A yuppie? I'd prefer a drag queen; they're more fun in bed. A yuppie drag queen? Never met one of those.

I was looking toward the window, my back almost to her. I felt her lean in, smelled the perfume. Hairs stood up on the back of my neck.

"Just a good, healthy American girl with a husky voice and the strength of a horse."

Green eyes, short hair. Louise Brooks nose, long neck. Going for a twenties look, except for the fully tattooed left arm. The arm closest to me. Here comes trouble, I thought. About time. Not much had happened since my last break-up. I caught her Bankhead reference, but I couldn't think of a comeback. I just looked and looked. The bartender brought the Oban. She opened her used-clothing-store purse but I reached over and closed it. Pulled out a bill and threw it on the bar.

"You sure? This stuff isn't cheap."

"I know. If you'd ordered McAllens I wouldn't have paid. I can afford Oban."

"Oban's better, no matter what they say. You come here often?" From her it didn't sound cliché.

"Only when I'm flush."

She smiled and, I swear, licked her lips. She was a bundle of clichés, but again, I wasn't noticing. Or maybe it's that in Berkeley we live with a different set of clichés. Here she was fresh. I looked her up and down and I wasn't too subtle. I usually go for healthier women, but I decided then and there that I needed a little decadence. A fairly short dress, pumps, 1930s body, no hint of a tan. We clinked glasses and she took a hearty slug, and I did too. I leaned back about six inches and thought to myself, well here we go.

Another Oban and more conversation, movies and books, life in Berkeley. She'd done the hipster circuit, Brooklyn, Silver Lake, a stint in New Orleans. Mission District till the yuppies moved in. Then a run in the upper Midwest. Currently living in the forties, off Broadway, near Mama's. North Oakland, but not the dreaded Rockridge. Just enough violent crime to keep things interesting. The bar was getting crowded so we had to lean close. Her lips tickled my ear. No more music but ears in lips and no more wit but tongues in ears. As the poet said.

She turned to face me, spread her arms wide. "So, what was your first impression?"

"Sexy as hell. But probably a fag hag."

"True on both counts. Guess I dress the part. Do you have anything against fag hags?"

"It can be difficult if there's an attraction."

A laugh, consisting of a single HA. "I'm not exclusively a fag hag. That would mean giving up sex. Do you know what Reich said about celibacy?"

"I can guess." She put her glass down, touching mine. Put her hands on my knees, leaned heavy. "I don't take you for queer."

"A little of both and everything in between."

"A man of experience."

"I like to try things."

5.

The lover and the beloved, the seducer and the seduced, I can play either end. I don't have strong sexual prejudices, it's all sex and I'll sink into any role that gets me there. Usually, though, I require more time. I like to savor the persona that I've chosen, or, rather, that the situation has called for. It takes some time to get past psychology, to get comfortable, to get to that place where it's all taste, smell and feel. It's all very Zen, I guess. But I hate that Buddhist crap.

It seems Grace liked picking 'em up in upscale bars and taking 'em home for a quick fuck. Getting comfortable wasn't an issue with her. She lived in one of those charming old places where nothing works, hallways that smell like old cologne and cigarettes, thread-bare carpets. Her studio apartment was fixed up nice, orange-umberish walls, Egon Schiele prints, a couple of photos of nude young boys in Sicily a hundred years ago. Fag hag. Heavy drapes. Everything brown, gold and muted orange. I sat on a striped couch: Ikea, but nice Ikea. She went into the kitchen, a separate room off the living area. Appeared with a bottle of Scotch. Something called Lagavulan.

"Don't worry. It's good."

It was good. Smooth and a little sweet, not much smoke.

She made one of those pre-sex visits to the bathroom. I scanned the two small bookshelves. Jackie Susann and some move bios. But also Terry Southern, Gore Vidal, Susan Sontag. No McSweeny's, no Paul Auster. I felt relieved. The only poetry was by Bertolt Brecht. Not bad.

It was a good ten minutes. I picked through *Blue Movie* looking for the raunchy parts, which was easy since most of the book is raunchy. There was a sentence about a perfect ass, then she came out of the bathroom wearing a robe that fit her style and the surroundings. Silk, I think. Bought in Tokyo. Did I like it? And she did a twirl, and I said, yes, very much.

She sat on the couch and we talked and kissed. Maybe it wasn't going to be the usual bang-bang after the bar encounter. She put Billy Holiday on the boom box. No rock'n'roll tonight. Fine with me. She moved away, a few inches. I pulled her toward me and her robe fell open. She seemed to like that. She had a smaller waist than I'd imagined, and smaller breasts. The boy-ish figure didn't go with the outfits, I'd expected a fuller look. Okay by me. She went limp and girly and I got the picture. She wanted manly. Bogy and Gary Cooper. I pulled and pushed and held her down by the shoulders. She didn't seem to want a lot of foreplay. Wanted to be taken. We'd come back around to one night stand sex.

A good healthy fuck and another scotch. More talk, mostly, thankfully, of things. Art and politics. She was smart and funny, had been around, was older than I'd thought, but not by much. Thirtyish. The great joy of the zipless fuck. Do people still use that term? Well, they should. I wasn't invited to spend the night. No hard feelings about that. I had a cup of coffee, let the scotch die down. Drove through North Oakland and back to the Chandler Apartments.

6.

Two strong cups of coffee and a little research on the screen. Jerry was born in Oklahoma City, raised by hard-working, God-fearing folks (aren't they all?). Dad was a plumber, but he died when Jerry Wally was in high school. He worked at a soda fountain to help make ends meet, bought the store, blah blah blah. Hard work. Praise the Lord and pass the homilies. Now employs over a hundred thousand workers, blah blah. I skipped the phony bio and found a couple of anti-Jerry sites, also the usual. Stiffs his employees, constantly being sued, buys politicians. None of the anti sites seemed especially nutty. I decided that the best way to serve old Drugstore Wally was to hit the streets, mingle with the people.

I drove the trusty Tercel down to Caffe Trieste, San Pablo and Dwight. It's a newish place, an east bay version of the old North Beach poetry haunt. Second best espresso in town. I noticed a few local celebrities as I waited to place my order. Maser and White, the rare book dealers, were parked at a back table. Probably discussing a deal. A couple of people from Good Vibrations, the dildo and lube emporium next door. Screeching pink hair and big belts. Nice to be in civilization, far from the suburbs.

I ordered a single espresso, known in the book trade as a pinky lifter. Sat by the window. Not much to look at on San Pablo. A liquor store, a junk shop. Some might think it quaint. I put on my detective face. Discreetly insouciant. Nothing happening. Not a clue in the house. I was about to get up when I saw a familiar face. Suit and tie, unkempt hair. Knew him from somewhere.

"Hello Clay. Care if I join you?" Jocko Belladonna. At least that's the name he goes by. Sometimes scout. Rumor has it that he worked for the IRS as an investigator. Or was it the FBI? I don't see him at library sales. He has some other sources. Gets good books, I hear. I nod; he goes for his pastry and a latte.

"I hear you're doing the private eye thing."

"Word gets around."

"What's the job?"

I figured he knew, but decided to keep some semblance of a cover. "Sort of a bodyguarding job."

A big guffaw from Jocko. Laughs so hard that his Allen Ginsberg style hair flairs out at the sides, Bozo style. "How much do you weigh? One forty? I hope you have a big gun."

"Somebody thought I could do the job. It pays the rent." A reference to scouting, which isn't paying well for any of us.

"Who do you work for?"

"That's classified for now."

"If you're working for a rich guy who is being harassed by a crazy Berkeley-ite, I may have something for you."

"For a price?"

"You get good books, Clay. Maybe we can do a library together sometime. Or something. I'll think of something."

Jocko's a little smarmy, but he's congenial. Sharing a library didn't seem so bad. I nodded.

"That guy Bruce, Loose Bruce."

"I know him."

"Well, this is third-hand. But I heard from Bruce that the crazy guy with the big white van…"

"Sasway?" Larry Sasway had a theory that came to him in a dream. It was Norman Mailer that killed the Kennedys, with help from Gore Vidal. A conspiracy of liberal quality lit authors. I couldn't remember the motive off-hand, but everybody in town has seen his big white van, decorated with pictures of Vidal, Mailer,

Sontag and James Baldwin wielding AK 47s.

"Yeah, Sasway. Bruce says that Sasway's got a new friend who has a thing for entrepreneurs."

"What made you think I'd be interested?"

"Berkeley's a small town, Clay."

Jocko finished his pastry and downed the last of the coffee. "Remember that library. And make it a good one."

I nodded and he left.

7.

I had a little bag of books, enough for lunch money, sitting by the door. I felt like socializing, and I was, after all, on a case. I took them down to Moe's.

I entered the store and dumped my books on the buy counter. Someone came around behind me and looked at me out of the corner of his eye. He'd been in the Trieste. Tall and lanky. Mystery eth? Black hair with a little artificial red. He went up to the second floor, pretending to browse. I was being followed.

Robert was the buyer. He takes his time, but the offers are pretty good. And he's good for a chat. A familiar face for twenty years or so. We talked about scouts past. We've been putting together a sort of hall of fame. Most of the stars are dead or getting too old for the game. Richie Favarito, the painter, hadn't been seen in awhile. Came up from Santa Cruz with box after box. Wore the best shirts! Designed, I believe, by his wife. Banana Box Bill, another scout who went for bulk. Two van loads a week, much of it junk. But when you hit pay dirt! All of them were full of stories, first editions that paid for trips to Vegas. The good ones can walk into a sale, go straight to the sellable book (do they smell them?), buy it cheap, and get out. Most of them read the books, too. Rogue intellectuals. A dying breed.

Robert took about half of the books and paid me enough for a light snack. I left the rejects behind the counter and went upstairs to find my shadow. He was looking at anthropology books, up by the front window. When he noticed me, he picked out a book. Obviously an amateur. Must be, if I can spot him. I haven't been doing this very long. Start to think; maybe all these crook types are obvious. Maybe I'm king of the detectives. I exited Moe's slowly so that he wouldn't lose me. Right on Dwight, up the stoop of the Chandler Apartments, home sweet home. I hid under the overhang till he came around, then threw a right, aiming for his adam's apple. A good target. He turned and ducked just in time and I caught forehead. Never underestimate the criminal element. He made the mistake of trying a kung fu stance. Didn't set up right and dug him under the ribs with my good hand. Hurt him but he didn't go down. We circled for a time, doing the old testosterone rag. Marvin came up behind him, on his way to cage a free drink from the rich detective. He got down on all fours and we did the old Three Stooges thing, I pushed hard and he hit the pavement hard, leading with his head. There were some oglers, but they all seemed too crazy to really care. I'm sure that worse things happen on their various home planets.

We dragged him upstairs and sat him in a chair. He was woozy but not quite on Queer Street. We got him some ice and asked some questions.

He gave his name as Metcalf and said that he would never squeal. Used that word, too. Marvin gave me a wink, said, Horst Buchholz, meaning, young and green. I went to the window and checked around for cops. The coast was clear.

"I'm told that a fall from six stories will kill you. I live on the fourth floor, but there's traffic. Four floors to the pavement, then an SUV. "

Horst-Metcalf shifted in his chair. Gave me a hard look. Shrugged.

I scooped up the cat and put her in the closet. She's a little window-dumb. Then I opened the window wide and pulled in the screen. Metcalf seemed pretty cool. Or maybe he was too dumb to know what was coming. Woozy? Marvin and I got on either side and lifted him out of the chair. He squirmed but he didn't really fight. He was wiry. Didn't weight much. We dangled him out of the window, holding his legs. A homeless person gave us the peace sign. You can get away with almost anything in South Berkeley.

"Who do you work for, slim?" Marvin was having fun with this.

"He gave his name as Cabot."

"Doesn't help us much. What's he look like? Where's he live?"

"C'mon guys." Guys?

"Hey, Metcalf, here comes a Golf. Do you think a compact would kill you? Or should we wait for something that's Ram Tough?"

"Don't tell the cops. I'm three strikes."

"Do we look like cops?" Come to think of it, I could probably pass. But Metcalf lets that go.

"Pull me up first? I'm dizzy."

We pulled him in and dumped him on the couch. "He's a big guy with a British accent. That's all I know. All I had to do was keep an eye on you."

Seems Jerry was keeping an eye on his investment. Cabot?

I was ready to let him go, but I was curious. "Metcalf, with all due respect, you don't seem like a hardened criminal. What were those other strikes?"

"Theft. I hit a register at a bookstore in Santa Cruz."

"And offense number two?"

"There are lots of registers."

Marvin smiled, wide and slow. "Hey Metcalf, we're in the book business, too."

8.

"Grace to be born and live as variously as possible." This from Marvin, said between quaffs of Bandol Rosé. I'd been telling him about Grace, a little at a time. Grilled chicken over greens and a loaf of potato rosemary bread.

His countenance grew dark and cloudy, as Conrad might say, and he looked at me with one-and-a-half bottle eyes. "Have you done the double?"

The fountain of youth, the myth of paradise, pie in the sky, the incredible double fuck. Easier now, with all the drugs. But I hadn't gotten around to those yet. I was still doing it on the natch, as was Marvin. To hear him tell it. Ten years my senior!

"Not yet, Marvin, but I think we'll get around to it."

He let out a hoot worthy of a frat boy on Coors. Poured another glass of that beautiful pink wine. "Keep me posted."

9.

I fell asleep with thoughts of Grace, slept well and called her first thing in the morning. I left a message for the whisky and cigarette voice. See me soon? Got dressed and walked down to the YMCA.

Two guys in the locker room were talking about gutting the president with a fishing knife. Jolly about it though. Berkeley. Went upstairs to do my workout but the Yoga people were having quiet time, and I like to sweat and grunt. Found a rowing machine away from the fray, or the lack of fray, and tried not to sweat too loudly. Decided to do some steam. There's a huge African-American guy with cornrows. Sits in the back. Practically lives there. I remember that Kerouac poem that goes, Charlie Parker looks like Buddha. This guy looks like Charlie Parker looking like Buddha. He was talking to a scrawny little guy wearing glasses. In the steam room. Nerd city. Says, "They put in some drug-store that looks like Pontiac Stadium and I'm going for my gun, son. Don't doubt me." The nerd nodded so hard that the glasses slid down his nose.

10.

Out on Shattuck Avenue, clean and healthy and the sun was shining, no sign of fog. Bruce was sitting in front of the movie theatre, cup in hand.

"Hi, Bruce. Anything you can tell me?"

"I had something to tell you."

"Remember what it was?"

"Ten dollars." He held out his hand and I gave him a five.

"That guy with the van gave me some good pot. I'm sleepy."

"That's not what you wanted to tell me." Legend has it that Bruce was a chemistry major at Cal in the sixties and got a little creative with the chemicals. But this is a story you hear a lot around Berkeley.

"Larry says that Terry says that the guy isn't real."

"Could you give me a little more, Bruce."

"Pot's better than crack. I feel pretty good."

"A little more. Who's Terry?"

"He's real old school. He's a Marxist-Leninist."

I hadn't heard that in awhile. Bruce pronounced the names slowly, with reverence.

"And who is the guy?"

"Drugstore Jerry. We're a gang, Clay."

The failure of communism, right here on Shattuck Avenue. "Drugstore Jerry is a phony?"

"That's what I'm saying."

11.

Bruce fell into a stupor before I could ask about Cabot. I decided to head home. Fed the cat (again) and checked my messages. Marvin, accepting my dinner invitation for that night. Then Haystack, or was it Cabot, sounding just like Sebastian Cabot, would I call him as soon as possible, or better still, come out to Orinda and see him at once?

I made myself a cup of coffee and took my time drinking. I'm not used to being ordered around. They pay the big bucks, they expect a slave. I thought about not showing at all. Then I said goodbye to the cat and found the Tercel.

Blasting hot in the suburbs. It wasn't a long ride, but it wasn't fun. I was sweating a lot by the time I got there. The porch was nicely shaded. I leaned my head against the wall before ringing the doorbell. I was enjoying the coolness of the prickly stucco when the door opened, a gush of AC. Haystack. I wondered if maybe he was a soccer thug. They must have day jobs.

Soccer thug/butler. There's an interesting life.

Haystack was sweating as much as me, AC not withstanding. He led me into the office. Drugstore Jerry was standing in front of his desk, leaning back. In a white suit, all silvery and backlit. In his manner, he put out his hand and pulled it back fast.

"I said I'd poke around for a couple of days. That gives me another half day."

"Maybe I misunderstood. Have you found anything?"

"A street person thinks you're two-faced, and if the Buddha sees you out on the road, he'll shoot you. And you may have something to do with Susan Sontag's part in the Kennedy murders. Aside from that, I'm coming up short."

He threw back his head and had a good laugh. The light played beautifully on his gray mane. Hair that rivals Michael McCLure! "Well, you certainly do associate with a colorful bunch. You know, I was once a bohemian myself, in my college days. Unfortunately I had to work for a living, and that gets in the way of all that. Then, there are the drugs. Of course, I disapprove of that."

I was hit with a wave of editorial comments but I dummied up. This guy was paying my rent, for now.

"Let's cut to the chase Mr. Blackburn. Do you have any real leads?"

Real leads mean real dollars. "I'm keeping a close eye on a couple of the local nut cases. Could turn into something."

"Does this mean you're in my employ?"

I swallowed hard and said yes. I felt a pang of longing for my days as a book scout. Damn you, Amazon. We made payment arrangements. He didn't seem to mind that I wanted half in cash as a tax dodge.

He offered me a drink, to celebrate. Decided to take him up on it. Maybe I'd learn something. He brought out a bottle of Cutty Sark. Cheap bastard. He did, however, have ice tongs. I like ice tongs.

"Detective Blackburn, tell me about some of your more colorful cases. You must have stories enough to fill a book."

I took a gulp of the so-so whisky. I could feel the surliness rising up my spine. My neck muscles got tight, my head ached. "Gee, Mr. Wally, let me see. I once watched a capitalist bitch fall out my window, only to be run down by an SUV."

"And what part did you play in this little adventure?"

"I stepped aside when she came at me with a ginzu knife."

"Did you do time for that?"

"Nope. Self defense." Something sounded wrong. My poet's ears detected something. It was the way he said *time*, referring of course to prison time. He didn't say it in quotes. There's a way that people use that phrase when they've actually done the time. Heavy, eyes down. Was Drugstore Wally an ex-con?

"What got you into the drug trade, Jerry? Does it go back to your bohemian days?"

"Not at all. It was the lunch counter. I love those places. The scent of grilled cheese, the coff—"

"What about the drugs?"

"Highly profitable. The country's getting older, Clay. I can sum up the future with one word. One word that will make the wise man rich. Do you know what that word is?"

"Plastic?"

He laughed and nodded knowingly. I guess he got the reference. "No, Clay. The word is—big stage whisper—*Lipitor.*"

12.

I fed the cat again and took a long hot post-suburb shower. It was foggy and cool in Berkeley. I went up to the roof half wet and felt the breeze. Grilled cheese and Lipitor. I was completely at sea. Over my head. But the checks were cashing. The poet side of my brain wasn't screaming yet. Working up to it, though. This guy drank bad whisky! How could I protect someone like that. And that stupid hairdo. God. The sun was low, and of the bright orange ball variety. I sat on a rusty lawn chair and let my poet's brain go its own way.

I was on a stake-out once. No, really. Me and Marvin and a thermos coffee, laced with El Presidente brandy. We talked all night, fogging the windows of a rental car. I often drift back to those conversations. An hour or so before dawn we hatched a theory that most presidential elections have been decided on the issue of hair. Best hair wins, beginning with Wendell Wilke.

Wilke had wings. Just couldn't plaster down the sides, and it looked real funny. Lost votes. Ike and Adlai were a toss-up, and in the event of a tie you look to the shape of the head. Stevenson's head was too round. It wasn't the debate that put JFK over. He beat Nixon, well, by a hair. Goldwater also suffered from those wings. No amount of Brilcream could keep his hair from flapping. Hubert Humphrey had the worst hair in American politics. Never had a chance. McGovern-Nixon was a festival of bad hair. Voter turnout must have been low that year. Jimmy Carter had some of the best hair since the days of Andrew Jackson. Still, he couldn't best Reagan's shoe polish job. Mondale tried to out Reagan Reagan, but he couldn't get the thickness. Dukakis broke the string. I'll never understand how he lost to Bush. I'd have bet my house on that sprayed black mass. With a coif like that I could rule the world. Clinton, always the smart politician, went for a slightly puffier Billy Graham look, and it served him well. Bush's hair isn't great, but Gore has wings of his own and Kerry's was too obvious. Palookas, both of them. Obama's clean cut personified his claims to change.

It was dark when a cool breeze brought me out of my reverie. I thought about Jerry Wally again. His hair. Something was wrong with his hair. I played our meetings over in my mind. The hairline was wrong. A rug? Possibly, but a good one. The breeze turned to wind and I went back downstairs, thinking deeply on hairdos.

13.

I was sitting at my desk and reading a Fielding Dawson short story. Stopped to rest my eyes. Out the window and across the street, above Shark's Used Clothing, they were at it again. For nearly a year, I'd had a Jimmy Stewart's eye view of the couple. She was kind of big, but not unpleasantly so. Lots of dark hair. Black Irish? He was a kind of wiry. They would start in the shower, the window on the left. I could only see heads and shoulders there. Soon they would move to the bedroom, where the window was almost floor to ceiling. I guess they weren't visible from the Avenue. Would have drawn a crowd. Brie, my downstairs neighbor, could also watch the show. She soon became bored with the lack of variety. Man on top, woman on the bottom, get it over with. Don't they do anything else? I didn't see it that way. After seeing them countless times I noticed small variations. And it was fun sex. Lots of tickling and towel snapping. I have a nice pair of opera glasses, and I used them on occasion, but I preferred to see them small, across the street and through the trees, almost golden in the afternoon light.

The cat was playing in the hall. I had left the door slightly ajar so that she could push her way back in. I heard a creak and assumed that was Emily, my prize tortoise-shell. Then footsteps, definitely not paws. I grabbed a book from the desk and turned. You can kill somebody with a book if you want to.

He was standing a few steps inside the apartment, me on the other side of the room. Scruffy and obviously crazy. I'm not completely familiar with the pecking order of the street sleepers, but there must be one. There's always a pecking order. This guy was at the bottom. The scent of urine and sweat filled the room. He was familiar. I'd probably stepped over him a hundred times, given or refused change, depending on my mood. Reagan let them out. It's a cliché in Berkeley, something you say when you see someone so hopeless that they should be under constant care. Reagan, Prop. 13, whatever. America's little Third World.

Sometimes crazy people make their way into the Chandler, but they usually sleep on the stairs. This guy was pretty bold. He looked at me, and, I think, smiled.

"Clay Blackburn?" He looked unsteady on his feet.

I stood up and nodded. Made ready to catch him.

"He gave me ten dollars to tell you something. But I can't get it wrong."

"Tell me."

"The drug guy isn't the drug guy." He closed his eyes, thinking hard. "Double trouble. More later." Punctuated with a self congratulating nod.

"What's that supposed to mean?"

"I dunno. Do you give me something, too?"

"Not unless you tell me who sent you."

"Not part of the deal." He looked confused. Me, too. I had a twenty in my pocket. Dug it out, offered it.

"Some guy that Bruce knows. I don't know him."

"What's he look like?"

"Big guy with a beard."

"What color?"

"White guy."

"The beard?"

"Oh, yeah. Gray. Gray beard."

"Where'd you meet him?"

"The street." I wasn't going to get my twenty's worth.

"So Santa approaches you and tells you to tell me this. Out of nowhere?" I was losing him. They can't tell what they don't know.

"I'll go now." He put out his hand and I gave him the twenty. Soft touch.

14.

Marvin leaned back in his chair and surveyed the post-dinner table. Mussel shells, mostly. Two empty wine bottles, dirty dishes, half-bottle of Jameson's. He righted himself then poured a little more whisky into a tumbler. Leaned back again. His bicycle pants were a shiny maroon. He was wearing a Chicago Bulls t-shirt, torn at the neck. He had been telling me stories about some adventures in Central America. I believed some of them. When I saw him like this, in his Neil Young drag, drifting on a belly full of good food and wine, it was hard to imagine him doing Marx's work in the jungle.

Between war stories we'd also discussed my case. I wasn't sure that he'd listened, he'd only responded with grunts and nods. But suddenly his eyes showed light and he was focused.

"Saddam!"

I assumed he was onto another story. I waited for the other shoe.

"Just like Saddam! Drugstore Jerry has doubles! There are probably scores of Drugstore Wallys, pressing the flesh and giving pep talks. One of your scruffy friends handed you a clue. Jerry isn't just two-faced. He's a different guy,"

"Jerry's features are pretty distinct."

"Don't you watch those make-over shows? They knock out your teeth, break your nose, suck out some fat and you look like Brad Pitt. The Docs could turn out a fleet of smarmy CEOs."

15.

I hit the streets early and checked all the usual places. Bruce wasn't in People's Park, wasn't in the obvious alleys and doorways. I asked around, nobody knew anything.

I approached a couple of hefty guys with gray beards but got no satisfaction. Mostly I got the bum's rush. Berkeley isn't always the friendliest town. I grabbed a mediocre piece of pizza and hung on the Avenue, asking questions that didn't get answered. The espresso guys, a couple of street vendors, the book clerks. Nope and double nope. I doubled back and sat in Ho Chi Minh Park. A great looking young man was playing Frisbee with his dog. I watched him with Walt

Whitman wonder. The miracle of bare legs. It was getting close to the cocktail hour, or close enough, so I walked up Telegraph, through campus, down to Shattuck Avenue and north to the gourmet ghetto. I wasn't going to Cesar's to run into Grace. You don't do that when, after a zipless fuck, you don't get a call back. Or maybe you do.

The bar was full. Usually when it's that crowded I walk out, but I was a little too tired to look for another place. I walked in and I was khaki deep in Blue Staters. It's hard to hate them, but it's also hard to care. I comforted myself with the fact that they wouldn't lynch anybody. There was one stool open at the bar. Well, almost open. I had to ask a business casual type to move her Cody's book bag. The bartender was a young guy, nerd chic with a knockout pair of fashion glasses. He was good, too. Caught my eye a few seconds after I'd gotten situated. I ordered a gin and tonic, not bothering to call the label. They use good stuff in their well drinks. I scanned the bar and she was there, at the far end by the bathrooms. Sharing a joke with the guy who fixes my Toyota. He waved hi and she caught my eye and lifted her drink. Got up and came over to me. I liked that a lot. Squeezed in close, inching out Ms. Business Casual. Kissed me full on the lips. Scent of scotch and perfume. Butterflies.

"What are you up to tonight?"

"I'm on a case." I still can't say this without feeling dumb. Maybe someday I should get a license.

"What do you do when you're on a case?"

"I sit in bars and cafés and talk to people."

"What do you do when you're not on a case?"

"Same thing. But when I'm on a case, I drink nicer cocktails. I'm on a retainer."

"Is this a murder case?"

"I'm protecting someone from bodily harm. If you can believe that." This got a chuckle. I'm barely 5'9"and weight just under one-fifty.

"What are your qualifications for this job?" When she said this she leaned forward and touched my forehead to hers. Oh god.

"I made it to the Golden Gloves semifinals in my home town."

"Welterweight?"

"You know the weight qualifications. I'm impressed. But I was a lightweight at the time."

"Well you're no lightweight now." She leaned closer, if that's possible. Sometimes obviousness is a blessing. "Have you had dinner?"

"I don't need dinner right away. Shall we go to the Chandler Apartments?"

Back through campus, down the avenue and into the elevator. A second fuck isn't a zipless fuck. Often it is better.

She didn't begin pumping me for information until after, thank God. I told her that these things had to be kept confidential. Something I learned from watching PI shows on TV. Actually I didn't much care about hanging Drugstore Wally out to dry, but I didn't want to let go of any info until I found out who she was working for.

I got up mid-question and went into the kitchen.

She followed me and peered into the reefer with me. I pulled out some cheese and a few olives. Half bottle of Tavel Rose. Directed her to the bread. Naked in the kitchen. Something very intimate in that. Two baby steps beyond the zipless. But was she a spy?

I looked her straight in the eyes. Tried not to show another erection. Butterflies again. "Why all the questions?"

"It's all very strange. Bookscout, yes. And most book nerds have artistic pretensions, so I get the poetry obsession. Detective doesn't follow. So I'm interested. What's the big deal? Do you think I'm a noir girl? Gonna chase you with a knife?"

"It happens."

A big role of the eyes. "C'mon. Tell me who you're protecting."

A tongue-in-my-mouth kiss, the kind that makes straight guys feel almost attractive. Luckily, I'm only half straight. I was able to resist spilling the beans.

"Hey, Clay Blackburn, can you do the double fuck?" Another kiss, her tongue cool from the chilled wine. She left a couple of hours later. Not ready to spend the night.

16.

Sometimes you see them in doorways. You're not sure if they're dead, sleeping, or in trouble. There's a judgment call whether you walk by or you call the police. Cops must get pretty sick of these calls.

No judgment call here. This guy was dead. I was exiting the Chandler on my way to the gym, nice sunny day, students walking by on the way to class. He was on the stoop, blocking the doorway. I stepped over him and touched his face. Cold. Definitely the guy that invaded my living room, even worse for wear. Terrible smell, but not too much worse than when he was alive. I checked his pockets for ID. There wasn't any. I dug the phone out of my gym bag and called the cops. Sat a few feet ahead of him, bottom step, where the air was almost fresh. There wouldn't be much investigation. I guessed that he was shot full of the latest low-end opiate. A little warning?

After the cops left, I went upstairs and took a long hot shower. I had been playing around the edges, spending my advance and having a little fun with the rich guy. Now I was in some real shit, possibly deep shit.

I dressed and put in a call to Marvin. I was going to need a little research, maybe some muscle. I went downstairs and hit the street. The cops were still wrapping things up. They eyed me as I left, but I didn't mind. They eye everybody. Part of their training. I found the Tercel, half block away on Regent. Tore up a parking ticket and headed down to Shattuck. Checked out Bruce's favorite corner. No go. I asked a couple of the street folks if they'd seen him. Blank looks.

Back into the Tercel and down to San Pablo, Café Trieste. Parking right out front. Something was going right. I ordered my espresso and found a seat. Two bites into my biscotti, Jocko came in, wearing a maroon shirt and a wide greenish tie. Light blue sport coat with kind of matching pants. I motioned him over. He ordered a large orange juice, came over and sat down. I described the dead guy. Not familiar. No, he hadn't seen Bruce. Not for days. He had seen Larry Sasway's van, though. Up San Pablo, near Solano. Less than an hour ago. I dumped two spoons of sugar into my pinky lifter and drank it fast. Excused myself and fired up the old Tercel. An illegal U-turn and I was pointed north on San Pablo, up toward Solano.

17.

Sometimes fate throws one a fish. I took a right on Solano and the van was there, a few blocks up, parked in front of a Tibetan Restaurant; and, miracle of miracles, there was a parking place on the same block. Too bad it was too early for my lunch. I could have gone for a yak burger. As it was, I stayed close to the van, window shopping and keeping eyes peeled for Larry Sasway.

He left the restaurant carrying a white paper bag decorated with the image of a prayer flag. I decided in a split second to play it tough. Larry's a little guy, with thick glasses and fifties style haircut, what used to be called a wiffle. I figured I could take him if I had to. I grabbed his bag.

"I hope this is a burger. I'm hungry!" Clay the bully.

"It's a potato thing. I don't eat meat." Larry gave me a look that could kill, except that it was cockeyed. He grabbed at the bag and I pulled it away, just in time. I know from my boxing days that you can anticipate a guy's next move if you watch his eyes. But Larry's eyes were weird. One seemed too big, due to the glasses. The other looked the wrong way, like Jack Elam. The weird eye slowly looked toward the heavens. A bird? A plane? I followed the eye with both of mine, and he caught me with a chopping left, flush on the chin. I have a tough chin. I didn't go down but it hurt like shit. He grabbed the bag, but it broke and the Tibetan potato thing landed on the sidewalk. I covered up and started my counter, but he ran to the van, around to the driver's side and got in. I followed. Another fish from the fates. The passenger side was open. I got in and grabbed his keys as he took them from his pocket.

"Okay Larry, I owe you lunch. But I had to act fast."

"Don't call me Larry. It's Lawrence. You're Clay Blackburn, the book guy. What do you have against me? Are you crazy?"

"Lawrence, with all due respect you're the guy that claims that Saul Bellow drove the getaway car after Gore Vidal shot Kennedy. I'm crazy?"

"Vidal was a decoy. Tennessee Williams fired the fatal shot. Why did you take my potato thing?"

"I'm a little rattled. Somebody was murdered and left on my stoop. And my pal Bruce is missing. I figured I'd get your attention. Then you sucker punched me."

A sly smile. "I've been using that eye fake since second grade. Buy me another potato thing and I'll point you to Bruce. Who got killed?"

"Don't know who got killed." I described the dead guy and got a quizzical look, although all of Lawrence's looks are slightly quizzical. "Lead me to Bruce and it's potatoes for you."

"He's been hanging out with a guy called Terry. Find Terry and you'll find Bruce."

"I hear you've been hanging with Terry."

"They didn't take me seriously. I have real information. There's big trouble ahead. I need to form a posse to take on the quality lit gang. They've killed so many."

"Aren't they getting a little old? Or dead? Sontag's not going to shoot anyone."

One eye looked to God, the other at the traffic. "They have young followers! Steinke! Lethem! Eggers! Heidi what's-her-name! I'm going to have to repaint my van."

"Before you get started on that could you tell me a little about Terry?"

Rolled his eyes. Every which way. "He's obsessed with the chain stores. He didn't put down my theories. But he didn't listen either. I thought he was listening at first."

"Does he have an address?"

"He used to have a place on Ashby, above Alcatel Liquors. I don't know if he's still there."

"What's he look like?"

"Do I get my potato thing soon?"

"Sure. What's he look like?"

"Bushy gray beard. Kind of athletic. Tan."

I gave Lawrence a few dollars for a Tibetan lunch and drove across town.

18.

Somebody told me that Lucia Berlin once lived there. It's a solid brick building, slightly down at the heels. The liquor store on the ground floor has been there for many years. Surprisingly good wine selection, considering the neighborhood. No Terry listed on what was left of a directory. I rang all five buzzers. No answer. I went into the store and bought a bottle of something called Lungarotti Rubesco, from a place called Torgiano. It wasn't too expensive and I liked the label. The clerk was a great looking tough girl with short, very black hair. No color in her tattoos. The straight stuff.

"I was supposed to meet a guy named Terry but he didn't show. White guy, gray beard, tan. Have you seen him?"

She smiled, and the smile said, this jerk's a cop, he gets nothing from me. "He comes around sometimes but I haven't seen him today."

"I'm not a cop or a bounty hunter or a repo man. I just want to say hello." I gave her one of my cards, the one with a phone number.

"Are you a detective?"

"I'm a poet."

She let out with a healthy, hooting laugh. She had crinkly blue eyes and a nice, Brigitte Bardot-type mouth. "There used to be a poet living upstairs. She was nice. But she didn't have a business card."

"We're coming up in the world."

"Alright, poet, I'll give you a little hint. Terry has a dog. Don't know how he slips that past the landlord. Nice looking black lab. Don't look for him across the street at the Petco. Terry hates chain stores. He could be at Red Hound, up on College. Or he could be out at the dog park, or at the Marina, walking Ezra. That's the lab. Hey," here she squinted at the card, "Clay... Blackburn? I think I have a friend you'd like. He's a poet. Do you do boys?"

"Depends. Feel free to show him the card." I left her laughing. Great laugh.

19.

It was one of those days when everybody looks great, just enough sun, tattoo and belly button weather, gym shorts to the café, so I wasn't surprised that the woman working at Red Hound was a knockout. I waded through two poodles and a mutt with a drooling problem, past the toy section, and asked my questions. Terry's description did register, but she hadn't seen him.

Next stop Berkeley Marina. I was on a parking run that was truly historic. I found a place down by the water, facing the Golden Gate. Had to fight the temptation to roll down the windows and just sit in the car for a few hours, waiting for sunset. I made myself exit the car and walked toward the part of the park that is reserved for dog walking. Frisbees were flying and dogs were everywhere. A nice wholesome scene. No gray-bearded men with black labs, however. I walked around for a while. Had a nice conversation with a Jack Russell. Found a bench facing the water and caught some sun. This detective stuff is hard work. I was almost asleep when I felt a wet nose on my arm. A black lab, but not the right black lab. The owner was an attractive, slightly hip looking woman, say, forty. Reeking of "professional." Nerve.com fodder. I smiled and returned to my reverie. That dog had no idea that he was a red herring.

After awhile I felt a strong need for a catfish burger. I went back to the car. As I got in, I saw a black lab jump into an old VW Rabbit. A man with a gray beard walked around to the driver's side, got in and drove off. How the fuck did I miss him?

I pulled out and got behind the Rabbit. I was tailing an out-of-date car in my out-of-date car. Who would win? I stayed back. Easy to be inconspicuous in a gray Toyota. He took a right on Sixth, past the Creative Arts building, then left on Dwight Way. All the way up Dwight. He slowed as he got closer to my apartment. Looking for parking? Looking for me.

I went up a block, left on Regent, down toward Ho Chi Min Park. Found a place a couple of blocks from home. As I walked back to Dwight, I spotted his car parked outside Bongo Burger. Fucker got a better spot than me. Didn't see him on the street so I assumed he'd be on the stoop. I was right. I braced myself for I-don't-know-what when he approached me. He shook my hand.

20.

"I'm Terry Olson. Figured you'd be looking for me. Are you a hit man?"

"No. I think I'm supposed to find you though. Were you threatening Drugstore Wally?"

"Hey, that's a good nickname. But Wally's not Wally."

I invited him upstairs. He asked for a bubbly water. I motioned him to the couch and poured him the drink. He looked a little like Dr. John. The face was a little too young and feminine, didn't match the beard and the booming voice. That stretched, plastic surgery look.

"Wally's me, Wally's everybody. Wally's the working man and woman, the down and out. He's anybody who needs a job!"

Shit. Another crazy guy. "We all know he's a smarmy

bastard, Terry. But is Wally Wally, in the real sense? Or are you speaking metaphorically?"

"Wally isn't Wally at all. In any sense of the word, Wally is not Wally."

I've lived in Berkeley for close to twenty years. Street folks, philosophy majors, aging radicals... Life in Berkeley can be one long version of who's on first. Being a poet I sort of like the game. Linguistic juggling is part of what I do. There was, however, a job to be done. I could turn this nut over to Wally, real or otherwise, collect the rest of my pay, and take a little trip down to Baja. Sun and sand, that's what I needed. My Spanish is terrible, but I probably communicate better down there. I was losing the plot up here.

"Terry, did you threaten to kill Wally?"

"The real Wally?"

"Any Wally. Any at all. Disney, Mathau, some guy up the street. Did you send threatening letters to a Wally?"

"Nobody did. That's a ruse. They just wanted to get to me. I'm going to expose them the right way. I'm a whistle blower, like Silkwood. Were you followed?"

Not that I'd noticed, but I'm still not very good on that point. Need more practice there. "Maybe. That would make sense. They follow me to you, and my job is over."

"I'm in disguise! And I'm in Berkeley! You're a trader. Those people are pigs. I thought you were old Berkeley!" He lunged at me and I sidestepped. He was nimble, didn't fall down. He swung and I caught arm, same side of the face that caught that last punch. I was going to be sore for days. I was pissed so I countered hard. Too hard. A nasty thunk, pain in my knuckles. I think I broke his eardrum. He went down, grabbing his face.

"I'll get you for this. Whose side are you on? Bruce said you're a poet. I came to you, to reason with you. I think you're a lackey for the chains."

That did hurt. I never shop the chains. "Okay, Terry, I'm listening. But stop the Wally-Wally. Make it plain, okay?"

"I worked for the real Wally in Arkedelphia, when he opened his third store. Store manager. No benefits but the pay wasn't too bad, for Arkedelphia. He was around a lot then, micromanaging. We got to be pretty friendly. This was before the books came out, before the lectures. When the win friends and influence people bit took off, he disappeared. Bigger fish to fry."

He became animated and his voice got deeper, more Wally-like. "Before anyone knew it, there were stores everywhere. I was pissed. I thought, as a veteran employee, that he could do something for me. At least make me a district manager. I wrote him a letter. Two days later, one of his people came to the store. They pointed out that I look a little like Wally. I was confused, of course. Who cares? So they offer me twice what a district manager makes to be a double. You know, to fool would-be assassins. Except that it took a little nip and tuck, a little something around the eyes. Surgery! Good benefits, though. And I got to fly business class."

It was a crazy story but I'd heard worse. "Sounds

like an, um, okay job. If that's what you like. Why are you on the outs with him?"

"Wally and his people decided that it would be more democratic if we made the same as the associates in the stores. We were paid the same as a senior cashier, which was quite a cut. No benefits to speak of. Of course, there was always the possibility of working your way up the ladder. We were in the security division so technically we could be part of the Spirit of '76 crew. They make real money. But that's a long shot when you're fifty and you've had your face altered to look like a famous snake oil salesman."

"So what happened?"

"I up and quit. But they wouldn't let me. Wouldn't look good. I'd signed a series of wavers that included a gag order. Why not? I liked the idea of working in security. Maybe they were afraid I'd go on *Nightline* or something. Who knows."

"So you grew a beard and went on the lam."

"And stopped using the sun lamp. Wally's pretty tan. Now I'm in deep shit, though. The Spirit of '76 crew will murder me for sure."

"What makes you think they'd go that far?"

"They'll go as far as they need to go. Who would question that? Didn't they kill Party Joe?"

"Party Joe?"

"The guy they left on your stoop. Everybody knows about that. I heard it from Julia Vinograd. I feel like I killed him. I shouldn't have gotten him involved. I didn't think they'd go that far but they did. Guess I'm next."

I was beginning to feel the heat. If this nutty story was true, I probably had a cadre of private cops waiting on the stoop of the Chandler. I went over to the window. Metcalf! Somehow I'd missed him. Is there a school for private detectives? I needed to take a class on detecting a tail. He was right there, across the street, in front of the Krishna Copy Center.

I pulled Terry over to the window, but not too close. "You know that guy?"

"He worked at the center."

"The center?"

"The place where they fixed my face. I thought he was the janitor. Guess he got bumped up to security. Probably made more sweeping floors."

"How much security do they have?"

"A private army. Don't you know? You lefties are so naïve. They own the world. I'm small potatoes to them. They probably only have a couple of Spirit of '76 people in town, along with a phony Wally."

"I've met Wally."

"Not real Wally. He's probably down in Palos Verdes. He has a nice house down there."

"Is that where the center is?"

"The center's on Katella, out in Anaheim. Corporate headquarters is in Orange County."

My head was swimming. I wanted to avoid a showdown, give myself some time to think. "I think you need a shave."

"No I don't. Besides, my face hurts."

I pulled him into the bathroom. Pulled out some scissors and a razor. "Maybe we can get you out of here incognito. Old Horst isn't so smart. Maybe we can smuggle you out. Do you have a place to stay?"

"I'm at the French Hotel till the money runs out."

"If they don't grab you on the way out, go there. I'll contact you."

It took him awhile to shave. Heavy beard. I found him a pair of cut-offs and a loud Hawaiian shirt left over from one of my Baja trips. Flip-flops and a Moe's book bag for his old clothes. He looked like George Hamilton crossed with the poet Peter Gizzi, on holiday in Honolulu. Hide in plain sight.

"I look goofy."

"It's a goofy neighborhood."

I waited five minutes and looked out the window. Horst was still waiting. Ten minutes later, Terry called from the French Hotel. He didn't think he'd been followed. But how was he to know?

I put in a call to Snorinda and left a message with French. Have Wally call me on my cell phone. Then I turned off my cell phone. I needed to check in, but I didn't want to talk to them just yet. I needed Marvin's help. He had access to all kinds of information. He's a renaissance man for our times. Computer nerd, hacker, soldier of fortune, poet and critic, proud owner of an Econoline van. Everything a book scout/detective could want.

He said he'd drop everything when I told him I was making risotto. I told him to give me a couple of hours. Dinner at eight. I drove down to Berkeley Bowl and got lucky with the lines. Fennel looked good, and there was some broccoli romanesco. Cute and good tasting. Hit the cheese counter for gorgonzola and romano. Decided against adding meat. The cheese and the stock would make it rich enough. Made my way up to the cashier. Only five people ahead of me. Two women were making out, front of the line. Berkeley!

The town was being good to me. Parking right out front. No dead bodies on the stoop. I shared the elevator with Dina from Amoeba Music, always a nice occurrence. The cat was pissed off. Had I forgotten her morning feeding? Didn't think so. Fed her again just in case. Then I zapped the frozen chicken stock and assembled the ingredients. I'd have everything ready for stirring when Marvin arrived. He can usually down two cocktails in the time it takes to stir the risotto. I needed to soften him up. I opened the Lungarotti Rubesco for a breathing. Figured it would need all the help it could get.

Marvin arrived, Kramer-like, on a bicycle. Didn't feel like parking the van. The bike rolled into my writing desk as he tried to dismount. When he picked up the cat, she immediately started purring. It always amazes me that animals like Marvin. He's so floppy and clumsy, yet somehow they aren't spooked.

He was, as usual, wearing bicycle pants and a sweatshirt. Today both were sort-of green, if that's a color. Hard to believe that he can beat people up. I've seen him do it and he's fierce.

He grabbed one of my Ikea folding chairs from the dining room table and brought it into the kitchen. As always, he would hold court while I cooked dinner. I didn't mind this at all.

"I have Boodles. Would you like a martini?"

"Let's drink it straight. Do you have lime?"

"Of course. Go to it. I've got to stir this thing."

He poured a couple of doubles and we were off. He was just back from NYC, where he'd spotted the guy who had us thrown out of a Galway Kinnell reading last summer. We were drinking Tunisian red in a North African place on Sixth Street and decided, just for giggles, to go see Kinnell at the 92nd Street Y. Marvin sprung for a cab uptown and before I knew it we were seated down front. Marvin holds many strings.

Galway came on in a white suit, which gave us a fit of the giggles. I blame the Tunisian stuff. It's considered terribly rude to giggle at the 92nd Street Y. That's a serious place. Kinnell came on all sonorous, like William Shatner playing a great poet. We started repeating his lines, softly at first, then louder. He'd boom out, "The dead shall be raised incorruptible," and we'd parrot it back to him. He didn't seem to notice, but the guy in back of us was steamed. He's somebody you see at readings in NYC, probably a poet himself. Who isn't? The final straw was the line, "fish market closed, the fishes gone into flesh," delivered with all the flare of a John Carradine. We stood up and blasted the line right back at old Galway, who still didn't notice. The guy in back of us found someone in authority and we were shown the door.

Marvin was doing a great Kinnell as we recalled the incident. I stopped stirring long enough to pick up my glass and toast him. I asked him what he'd been doing in New York but he clammed up. Lefty stuff. Still a few anarchists in the old town. I wondered how they afford the rents.

The stirring was over and we adjourned to the table. I quickly dressed some greens and poured the wine. It wasn't bad. Score one for Alcatel Liquors. Marvin sniffed and tasted, then nodded. Then he dug into the rice and nodded some more.

I brought him up to speed regarding the Jerry Wally case. I tried to keep the story amusing. Crazy Bruce, the potato thing, it was all just a lark. Would he mind helping out? For Terry? He seemed like an okay guy.

"What have you found about about the homeless guy?"

"Not much yet."

"Might tell you something."

"Good point. I'd hate to do it but maybe I should call the cops."

Marvin rolled his eyes. He enjoys characterizing me as a babe in the woods. "Cops won't know shit. They never do. Call that transgender person. You know, the Fed."

I had always thought of Bailey Dao as a woman, but I let that go. Maybe Marvin knew something that I didn't. She did in fact work for the FBI, out of the local office. Agent Dao had gotten me out of a jam and I had done her a few favors. I couldn't remember who owed whom.

"I'll give Bailey a call. Are you on board?"

"With conditions. First, don't let Dao know I'm

involved. I have to keep my low profile. Why add to my FBI file? Second, I get to carry my gun."

"I hate those things."

"Fuck that. It's time to shed those bourgeois liberal ideas about gun control. Guns are as American as cherry pie. What's for dessert?"

"Dates baked in filo with a cinnamon cream sauce. So wear the gun. But don't use it unless the situation is dire."

"I understand the rules of engagement. My own rule is, shoot anybody to the right of Howard Dean and proceed from there, but I'll go a little easy, just for you. And there's one more condition."

"Whatever you say. I need the help."

"You have to tell me. Have you done the double with Tallulah?"

"You mean Grace."

"Well?"

"I don't usually kiss and tell."

"Bullshit."

"Yes, on the second night. Actually it was early in the morning, after the scotch had worn off."

"She's dangerous, you know." Said with a smile and a nod.

"She does ask questions."

"Probably works for Drugstore Wally."

"I'm not so sure. Maybe she's just curious."

"She acts like a noir character, which means she likes to think of herself as a femme fatale. She's right out of James M. Cain. She's the kind of woman that would convince you to kill your wife, if you had one."

"I think it's all for show."

"Don't be so sure. If it walks like a duck and quacks like a duck, sometimes it's a duck."

21.

I felt better with Marvin backing me up. I was worried about gunplay though. I'd managed to avoid shootouts in my short career as a "private asshole." Guns put little holes in people. Makes me squeamish. Also, it's harder to keep a low profile when you're spraying the area, any area, with bullets. My motto is, no license, no publicity, no cops. With the exception of Bailey Dao.

Marvin left before eleven. Said he had to do some work later. I asked him to keep an eye on the French Hotel. He said he would.

Haystack had left a message on my cell. The boss wanted to see me asap. Decided it was too late to do anything about that. I cleaned up the kitchen and poured myself a small scotch. Picked up a copy of Edward Dorn's *Gunslinger*, possibly my favorite all-time book. I've read it from cover-to-cover more than once. Now I use it is a sort of *I Ching*. I let it fall open and I read a few lines to see what *Gunslinger* has to say. I sat on the couch. Put my scotch on the table, next to the stereo. The cat jumped up and took a sniff. Scampered. Not quite the perfect companion. If only they drank scotch, I wouldn't need friends. I folded my legs and sat the book on my lap. I have many editions of the poem.

This was a newish one, from Duke University. Cloth, nice heft to it. I coaxed the book open, somewhere in the middle:

> Cool dry,
> Shall come the results of inquiry
> out of the lark's throat
> oh, people of the coming stage
> out of the lark's throat
> loom the hoodoos

A lark or a duck? And the phone rang, just like that. Her voice seemed even smokier than remembered.

"Hello, Clay Blackburn. This is a booty call."

That particular phrase had never been applied to me. I liked it. "I'm home. Nursing a glass of Glenfiddich. Will that do?

"You're not drunk are you?"

"Not especially. A little wine with dinner. Does it matter?"

"Want you at your best. I want that thing."

"Thing?"

"Up, down, and up again. Without exiting. You know."

"The incredible double fuck?"

"Is that what you call it?"

"Your first time?"

"Don't flatter yourself. It's rare but not unheard of. And I do have a thing for young boys. It comes pretty natural to them. Actually, old man, you're an exception for me."

"Maybe you should hurry on over before I forget what I like about you. My memory's not what it used to be. Where are you?"

"Look out the window."

She was across the street, in front of the skateboard store. She was wearing jeans and a man's sport coat. I waved and she waved back. Opened the coat. Predictably, she was naked under the coat. Sometimes predictable isn't so bad.

I met her halfway down the stairs. I noticed that she didn't have a purse or overnight bag. Strange for booty calls. We embraced and I felt some bulk in her suit coat pocket. Guess that was her overnight bag. Then I wasn't noticing anything, and we were on the old futon.

I have never done the double with such ease. Had I been twenty, I could have done a triple. I wonder who holds the record. Some porn star, no doubt. Sometimes everything is perfect. London poet Jules Mann once described a woman that she had met briefly in an airport. Her perfect sexual match. And she knew it, though it was never consummated. She probably still keeps that woman in her sex memory, years later. The poet Patrick Donegan calls this the 'Tadzio effect'. A perfect lust that you would follow to your death.

She wasn't on the beach, down by the water and she wasn't waiting to pick up her baggage. I was on top of her and we were fucking and fucking.

And then I was sitting up, leaning against the wall. She was in my arms, in front of me. No blankets left on the bed. Cigarette time but I don't smoke much anymore. I said to myself, I will count to ten and she will ask me a question about the case. If Marvin is right. Ten came and went and I thought, Hah, Marvin is wrong. At about twenty, she began to nibble at the edges.

"You lead a strange life, Clay."

God. that voice. "Not many book scouts around anymore, I guess."

"I don't mean that. The detective stuff. Tell me some thrilling stories about the case you're working on."

"This case is vexing me. Mostly I don't understand why Drugstore Wally is hiring amateurs. Am I so small time that I only rate three amateur employees? Where's the Spirit of '76 bunch?"

"What three employees?"

"There's the guy we call Horst. Metcalf's his real name. Haystack the butler. And you. You're a real pro in some areas, dear, but you're a terrible spy."

She flew out of bed and stood up. Fixed me with a good stare. I admired her flare for the dramatic. I hadn't dropped the blinds, and the streetlights on Dwight provided the perfect light. She stood so straight that she seemed to bend backward, and the light hit her shoulders hard but barely lit her face. God.

I rolled onto my stomach to avoid changing the subject. "Where'd he find you guys? He can't be paying much." She started to cry. No sobbing though. Her jaw was fixed tight and her eyes were still on me, albeit teary eyed.

"Listen, prick. I was an English major. I had a shit job in one of his stores. Owlblight, Wisconsin. Ever heard of that town? Had to move there because my aunt owned an apartment building. Cheap rent. I was an assistant manager. Nights, weekends, not enough pay to ever get out. Then the meat cutters went union. Two days after the union election, Wally closed the store. Pretty much put the town out of business. I applied for a job at the Drugs and More in New Cheapside, a twenty mile commute. I was home, waiting for the call and a couple of people from Spirit of '76 offered me a special assignment. If this works out, I'll get a middle management spot. Full health benefits. What could I do? But I can't do this anymore. I like you, and I like Berkeley. God, you can read! And you don't weigh three hundred pounds, and you don't wear an owl hat."

"Owl hat?"

"The local high school team, the Owlsblight Owls. They're a big deal up there. God, I hate men. But you're kind of different."

"You seem pretty sophisticated for an Owlsblight girl."

"I write a blog. And I did my thesis on Thomas Hardy."

And she throws a good fuck, I wanted to say but didn't. Mind on the job.

"Do you know about Metcalf?"

"No, but they said they'd be following me, for my protection. I took it as a threat. They can be pretty pushy."

"What would it take for me to hire you as a double agent?"

"A middle management job doesn't buy much loyalty. I mostly came down here to get out of Owlblight.

They flew me down business class! If you could find me an affordable rent in the Bay Area, maybe a job in a bookstore, I'd probably come around. And maybe a couple more dates, to see where that leads… and dinner at Chez Panise, downstairs."

"I can't afford downstairs, and affordable rents are hard to come by. What if I promise to do my best?"

"And the dates?"

"You're on. We'll start this week. I'm going to a reading Friday. Would you like to join me?"

"Beats anything that's going on in Wisconsin. Why not?"

22.

Michael Swindle was reading at Book Zoo, down the street from the Chandler. I'd have a couple of days to cool off and think before seeing her. Grace would come by at about 5pm. I had a vague plan for putting the squeeze on Metcalf if he followed me again.

I had some time to kill. I was planning a trip to the roof for a little sun when the phone rang. My phone is hooked up with the front door. Ring my number and the phone rings. A strange system, but useful. Turn off the phone and, voila, nobody home. This time I picked up, and it was Bailey Dao. I buzzed her in.

I opened the door and she strode into the middle of the room. FBI training. See as much as you can without a warrant. She is very tall. Mystery eth. Once described herself as Filipina-African with an Irish jaw. Left arm a sleeve of tattoos by Don Ed Hardy. Marvelous work, sailors and crosses and hearts. Jet black hair, cropped short. A force of nature. It is a good thing that we are no longer allowed to describe people as noble savages. And yet…

She kissed me full on the lips. I was shocked. I usually got a stiff, official handshake. "Hello, Ms. Dao. How's life with the Feds?"

"They cut me loose. Yours was the last call before they turned off my voice-mail."

"That's quite a surprise."

"They wanted me to state my gender. Or re-state. Or something. I told them it's none of their business. Besides, I'm in a state of flux right now. I could answer that question a couple of different ways. Like that has anything to do with my job! These neo-cons will be the death of all of us. And if you think they've gone away you're an idiot. "

"What will you do for a living?"

"I'm working your side of the street now. Going to get a license and everything." She reached into her jeans and brought out a card. I hadn't noticed before, but her clothes were more casual. No more cheap business suits.

Silhouette of a woman with a gun. Bailey Dao, Private Investigator. "Looks good. But the gun may be heavy handed. Mostly we spy on people. For that it helps to have a low profile."

"Don't worry, that's my joke card. Got another one for real clients. So, are we partners on this case?"

"I'm flattered that you'd ask, but I still work with Marvin. I was hoping to hit you up for some inside information, but it seems you're no longer on the inside."

"I'm still dating agent Lazari, so I can get into files, stuff like that."

Was Lazari male or female? Couldn't remember, decided not to ask.

"Are you on a retainer?" She was going to want money.

"Barely making expenses."

"By expenses you mean Negronis made with the best gin, high end restaurants, cases of Tavel..."

"Yeah. Like I said. Expenses."

"I'll see what I can do, then we'll negotiate."

I didn't like the sound of that but I went for it anyway. She's good at what she does. I filled her in on all the details. She tried to tussle my hair, but it was more of a rub since I keep my hair very short. Then another peck on the lips and she was on her way.

23.

I phoned the French Hotel. He wasn't in his room. I called the café in what passes for a lobby and described Terry. Not there. I called Marvin's cell.

"He's in the Elephant Pharmacy buying St. John's Wort. I'm just out of earshot, stocking up on shaving supplies. There's a sale. "

Marvin shaves every third or fourth day and when he does, he goes first class.

"Why don't you hop in your little car and meet us here? We'll probably be checking out in ten. We can go over to Cesar's for a drinky-poo."

"Why not." The Elephant Pharmacy is a hippie chain corner drugstore. Herbs, chair message, nutrition classes. Disgusting, but the prices are pretty good and the clerks are cute, in a new-agey sort of way.

I drove the Tercel into the lot and got a space first thing. Uncanny. The gods were with me. The automatic doors opened and I was hit with a wave of patchouli and sage. Not exactly perfume, scotch, and cigarettes. I tried not to inhale too deeply. Marvin and Terry were at the checkout. Perfect timing. I could taste the Negronis.

"Drinky-poos!" This from Marvin, with a little too much volume. So much enthusiasm for a man his age. Terry looked a little scared. It's hard to know how to take Marvin at first.

I knew when we left the store that there was trouble. We cut left toward the Econoline, parked next to the Tercel. Three guys and a woman exited a black Taurus. They'd found a space, too. Amazing. The woman looked like Hilary Swank in thug drag. Probably a yuppie, I thought. Until she kicked me in the knee. Caught us all off guard.

I countered with a lame right that she blocked. Marvin opened the van and pushed Terry in. Meanwhile I took another one for the team, a chopping left from one of her friends. Marvin fished around in his sweatshirt, where was that gun? But he was a little slow and they all drew. We were fucked. Terry was hustled into the Taurus and we were left looking like fools.

Marvin wanted to follow them but I had what I thought was a better idea. We barreled up 24 and through the tunnel. We got to the house in Snorinda in about fifteen minutes, record time.

I could hobble up to the house but I couldn't kick the door. Marvin rolled his eyes and did it himself. It was a tough door. Didn't budge. Marvin fished out the gun. I backed off and covered my ears. I hate those things. He shot the knob, well, the door really, off. Someday he'll do this and I'll catch ricochet.

"Marvin you fucker! There are easier ways to do that."

"But this is the fastest, gimpy." He pushed the door open. Empty house. No furniture, no Franz Kline. No bottles at the bar. We checked.

The place was easy to search. Bare floors. Not much else. We walked in the walk-ins and we checked the cupboards. Lots of shrugs. Went out into the yard. Nice yard. Marvin sat on the grass and pulled out his pipe.

"Do you think this is the right time for that?"

"Helps me think. Did you call Dao?"

"A couple of times." He offered me the pipe. I don't smoke much, but my knee hurt like shit. Not the first time I'd taken a hit there. I took the pipe.

24.

I spent the rest of the day climbing various phone trees, trying to reach Jerry Wally at Jerry's Drugs and More. Bailey Dao left a message. She was on the case. Hope she didn't expect payment. I was now working against my employer. Not very lucrative, but more comfortable, at least for me. Marvin loved it. The revolution and all. He didn't do this stuff for the money. He made enough at his day job. He was involved in this for, as he said, the pure fuck of it. Wanted to get himself a CEO.

I needed the kind of information that you can't get from a Google search, and all I could do was wait. I went downstairs and around the corner to BayKing for a donut. I checked out the poetry section at Moe's. Decided to do some book scouting. What else was there to do?

I've been a book bum since I dropped out of college, twenty-some years ago. I've worked in chain stores, in one-man operations, and everything in between. I owned a store in Santa Cruz called Campion's, out on Soquel Avenue near the movie theatre. I've scouted books all along. The Goodwill, estate sales, whatever. At this point I don't know what else I'd do. I sort of take it for granted that the detective thing will dry out. I'm not inclined to do it forever.

I went home to the Chandler, up the antique elevator to the fourth floor. Said hi to the cat and went into the kitchen. There's a false bottom in one of the cupboards. I pulled out my stash of bills. Not that many.

I'd been living well. I grabbed off a few twenties.

The Tercel was pretty close by. More good luck. I pointed it toward San Pablo, left toward Emeryville. There's an especially trashy little second-hand store down there. Proprietor's a real character. Bob Kelly. Slim Pickens type, and there's always a friend with him, shooting the shit. Today's pal looked like Mississippi John Hurt. If you stopped to count his wrinkles you'd be held up for hours. For some reason I was tempted to do just that.

"Clay Blackburn, poet detective. I've got books for you." He motioned to his book section, a scuffed-up old pine bookcase. I nodded hello and went to the case. Bibles! I can always turn over bibles. I picked out seven, all except the one that was stolen from a hotel room. They were in good shape. Bibles seldom look read.

"The word of the Lord, yes, sir." John Hurt nodded, looked serious.

"Five bucks per, Clay. These are nice. Leather!" He grabbed one from me and smelled it. "Rich Corinthian leather." Said with a phony accent. A phlegmy laugh from John Hurt.

I'd be lucky to make three apiece in today's book economy. "Ten for the stack, Bob. I can't get much for those."

"Tell you what. You go across the street to the Black Muslim's and get us a couple of muffins, then to the market for a couple of Millers. Good combination. That and the ten buys you a stack of good books."

I took the deal. Went across the street and bought muffins from the polite young man in white shirt and skinny tie. I was in the liquor store when the phone rang. Grace.

"It's Friday. What time are you picking me up?"

I'd forgotten, but it was only 2:30. Plenty of time to get to the reading.

"I'll see you in three hours."

"What does one wear to a poetry reading?"

"Is this your first?"

"I saw Robert Pinsky in college."

"Then it is your first. Wear whatever you like, nobody pays attention."

"Thanks, Clay."

"To your clothes, I mean. You'll get plenty of attention. I've never met a poet who wasn't on the sniff."

I bought the Millers, crossed the street and made the deal. Put my copies of the good book in the shopping bag. They had heft, smelled good, meant good reading to somebody, somewhere. Best of all, there was one non-bible in the bunch, a boxed edition of *The History of Tom Jones*. Still, these books would bring in chicken feed. I'd have to find another way to make a living. A detective's license? Hard to imagine. Maybe with Dao as a front...

I had a little less than three hours to kill. I pulled out the cell, left messages with Bailey and Marvin. I would have followed up some leads but I couldn't think of any. Besides, I had that copy of Tom Jones. I drove down to the marina, past Trader Vic's, past the Watergate Apartments, and found a parking place facing the Golden Gate. A cool wind was kicking up so I stayed in the car. I rescued Tom Jones from beneath the bibles. That Wesleyan University Press edition, edited by Battestin and Bowers, is the one I know best, although I've read the book a few times, including once on a plane to Dalien, China, in a lurid pocket edition from the sixties.

I decided to use the book the way I use *Gunslinger*, the way others use the *I Ching*. Art is my religion. Why not? Does all the same things that God does, and is a lot less destructive... "I was second to none of the Company in any acts of Debauchery; nay, I soon distinguished myself so notably in all Riots and Disorders... as I have addicted myself more and more to loose pleasure..." For the sheer fuck of it. This from Marvin, or a Marvin-like voice in my head, not from Henry Fielding, though it could be, in spirit.

I had distinguished myself in all riots and disorders, but I was still nibbling around this case. I once lit a cop car on fire, with Marvin's help. We were able to get away and when we were at a safe distance, we stopped for a drink. About two thirds of the way into my Negroni, I had an attack of the postmodern heebie-jeebies. How on earth would this help the revolution? What revolution? Could any good come of this? I turned to Marvin with my questions, but before I opened my mouth, he said, "For the fuck of it. For the sheer fuck of it."

I got out of the car and felt the cool, no, cold breeze. Litter was flying around, Candlestick Park style. Sometimes I hate the wind off the bay, but it does keep things clean. I walked along the water, covering my left ear against the wind. I began to tear up a little, which seemed dumb but then it didn't. I'd been nibbling around. It was time to get to the bottom of this rather absurd mystery. Time to throw caution to the, um, wind. Wreak a little havoc on some CEO. For the sheer fuck of it.

For now, though, I was almost late for a date. Grace lived close, so I was within minutes of being on time.

25.

Walking with Grace out to the car, I felt a mixture of intense lust and, I'll admit it, male pride. Dressed down and de-baubled, in poetry reading black, straight-stuff perfect, the toughness of her walk and her demeanor took front and center.

"We could just go to the Chandler. Forget the reading."

"You're being too obvious, Clay. We'll do the reading first."

I reached into my pocket and turned off my phone, got into the Tercel and we were off. No distractions tonight. I'd decided to pull a switch. The Charles Bernstein talk at SF State that night just wouldn't do it, even though it was the event of the poetry season. Something having to do with Zukovsky and western philosophy, as seen through the ever-expanding ether of the post-poet permafrost of a warming globe. Heady stuff, but not very sexy. That's why I had decided instead to stay in the east bay. Michael

Swindle at book zoo, very Boho. She didn't mind either way, was possibly relieved. Bernstein would probably be a snore, even for an English major. As I drove up Telegraph we talked a little about books and current events, and for some unknown reason, Beethoven's Late Quartets. I'd never thought of those pieces as sexy. I do now.

I liked the way her mouth looked when she formed certain words. I liked the third tattoo up from the elbow though I couldn't quite make out what it was. It was a light blue. Her skin was very white. Once, waiting for the light at Ashby, I looked at her collarbone against the black of her t-shirt, and half closed my eyes as if I were protecting them from glare. For this I got a confused look and "Are you all right?"

"I'm smitten."

"God. Poets."

I parked at the Chandler and we walked back to the strange little alcove of a mall, somebody's mid-seventies idea of a themed shopping center, the theme long forgotten. There were remnants of a palm laden south sea shack look, but only remnants. The anchor business was and still is a fondue place. Good God.

Book Zoo is all the way back of the semi-covered building. Closet sized, but stuffed with weird and interesting books. Swindle, the guest of honor, was drinking a beer in the doorway.

"How's the tour?"

"Low-budget fun. But I'm starting to miss New Orleans."

Nice drawl, I thought. I'd read a couple of his pieces

in the Village Voice, figured he'd do a fun reading. I looked around him into the store. Eric, the proprietor, was opening bottles of two-buck-chuck, nothing but the best. Leonard Cohen's first album was, I swear, playing on a turntable next to the register. Berkeley.

There are a few of these places left. Maybe they'll survive the mid-sized independents, since the overhead is low and the proceeds only need to feed a couple of mouths. I went over a mental list of these strange little places. Austin, Boulder, Boston. I hear there's one in Brooklyn. Places where I've done readings or sold a few books to pay for gas and lunch.

We walked in and found a place on the carpet, all eyes on Grace. We leaned on a shelf of old John D. Macdonald pulp. America's greatest gift to literature, next to Jackie Susann. Grace moved left and I shifted right and our sides were touching.

The audience arrived, tatooed and scruffy, save for a few Berkeley lit types. Barry Gifford, John McBride, Julia Vinograd. The under-the-radar crowd. Eric brought us wine before starting the show with a rambling introduction. Swindle, sitting in a well-worn easy chair, seemed to be dozing. He woke up and read stories about life in the Deep South: NASCAR, hound dogs, much drinking. Aside from the drinking, it was news from another planet. The Berkeley kids took it all in and laughed at the right time. There was a smoke/drink break, then another and another. The stories went on. I looked for signs of boredom from Grace, but she seemed happily involved. I was impressed.

Swindle finished his last story, something having to do with the Zapatistas, and a Patti Smith record came on. A turntable!

I paid my respects to the reader and his friends, anxious to get Grace back to the Chandler for some post-reading nookie. We hit the street giggling, our sides touching, finishing off the last of our wine. Top of the world, the pure laser of lust pushing at our extremities, even the street lamps pumped out a flattering light. A black Land Rover rolled by real slow, windows down, playing, of all things, a Steely Dan song, "Babylon Sister." I felt a little defensive, for a second. Hadn't I seen that car before? With that guy driving? But then the feeling passed and I was back in the moment. Go for the cotton candy.

The breeze had died away, leaving a very warm night; if we get more than a week like this in a year, we're lucky. Thought about warm parts of the world that I've been to, Mexico, Sicily, Honolulu. People half dressed on the avenue, drinking and hanging out on the little triangle park across from the Chandler. It would be noisy in the apartment tonight, but who needs sleep.

We were half undressed by the time the elevator reached the fourth floor. Made the front door, fed the cats, fast. Fell onto the couch. Everything moist and matted, hot weather sex. Somehow down on the floor when we finally got down to fucking, background music coming from the triangle, some hip-hop thing. Up the hill, then down again like roller coaster, that roller coaster feeling in the groin, then up again... the double fuck, then down again, going down. Then a conga, somebody in the park. Made us giggle.

"How do you sleep here?"

"It gets real quiet around 3am. Besides I don't need much sleep."

I'm usually real good at subtly turning off the phone. Nothing subtle about tonight's entrance. It rang, I didn't get it. I'd turned my cell off before the reading. They'd call back. We were close, relaxing. Fuck the phone. It rang again. I rolled over, got off the floor and picked up.

Bailey Dao. "Hey, fucker. Don't ever turn off the cell when we're working on a case. That's completely unprofessional."

"So I'm only a semi-pro. What's up?"

"The cops have Terry's body. I'm at the Emeryville Marina. Get here fast, but park in the Chinese restaurant and walk out to the pier. Stay clear of the cops. They're going to question you at some point, but let's not rush it. Let me handle things."

A control freak, and he/she is bigger than me. Some partner. I dressed, reluctantly, and left Grace to sleep in my bed.

26.

I walked down Dwight to the car. The bagpipe guy was on the triangle, inflating the bag in preparation for another rendition of "Amazing Grace." He was late this night. His usual routine involves marching down the street to the Café Med and ordering a coffee. It was past midnight, the Med was closed. The wind hadn't come back but the fog was in, and "Amazing Grace" felt especially soulful to me, for the obvious reason.

I found the Tercel and it sounded pretty rough. Time for a new muffler, perhaps a tune-up. Put it in gear and pointed toward Emeryville, past warehouses, high crime districts, and live-work yuppie hutches. The marina was almost fogged in. I parked in the lot of the giant Dim Sum house at the water's edge. Walked toward the blinking red lights. I didn't really hide, but I stayed behind some bushes. I spotted Bailey and she answered my wave.

Bailey Dao crossed over to the bay side of the break. She was wearing a black turtleneck, extra long, and black jeans that had been tailored. One red streak in her short very black hair. She's the kind of presence that makes you forget to breathe, sometimes for a couple of breaths. She looked at me the way I imagine she would look at a bug, but I took no offense. She probably learned that at the FBI school.

"They didn't weight him down much. Assuming they're pros, they probably wanted him to be discovered."

"They're trying to keep a lid on some folks."

"Why?"

"Something to do with plastic surgery."

"Using doubles as body guards? That would be a minor scandal. This is some serious damage control."

I was stumped. "You're the Fed. What do you think."

"We need to talk to your ex-cashier."

"I've talked to her."

"Between humps. Try it with your clothes on."

"Jealous?"

"You're not my type. I kind of like your partner, though."

A couple of detectives came over, flashlights flashing. In case there's some question, they really do wear cheap suits. Bailey gave me a look that said let me do the talking. And so I did. I nodded, smiled, shucked and jived. After a few questions, they seemed satisfied that I was an idiot and flashed their way back to the car.

Bailey shooed me away and I got into the Tercel.

27.

I was barely out of the Marina, Watergate Apartments and Holiday Inn to my left, when the cell rang. Bailey: "Wait for me at your place. I'll ask a few more questions, then I'll be at your door."

Entering my place I noticed a piece of paper on the floor. Nice note from Grace. She felt like sleeping at home, took a cab.

It was late, almost early, when Bailey marched into my apartment. I have some Christmas lights around my dining area. That was all the light I needed, mixed with the streetlight, almost at window level. The cat was sacked out on the couch. Bailey startled her and she ran like hell. Bailey didn't notice. She went straight to my closet and fished out a white T. Took off her black shirt and wiped off the sweat. Small but decidedly female breasts. A solid wall of muscle, beautiful brown. Sunbather? She hesitated while I gawked but she didn't smile. Put my t-shirt on. Too small, but in a good way.

"Do you mind, partner?"

"Not at all, but I didn't know we were that close."

"We can talk about that later. Let's get Marvin over here and put our heads together."

"Marvin will be sleeping."

"Somebody just got murdered. He can wake up for that."

Marvin picked up halfway through his message. "Fuck you, I'm tired. I bought books today. Remember book scouting? A stack of Harry Potters from some dumb kid, possibly stolen, and three boxes of Lit. So who got murdered?"

Good long silence on the phone. He'd be right over.

It wasn't quite early enough to call it morning drinking, so I pulled out a bottle of Campo Azul and poured myself a shot. I offered the bottle and a glass to Bailey. She took a pull off the bottle before pouring herself a generous shot.

"J. Edgar Hoover used to drink this stuff."

"Really?" I was pretty sleepy.

She rolled her eyes and snorted. "You're a putz, Clay. But I like saving your ass. What happened to your boyfriend?"

"Dino's down in Columbia, I think."

"A walking bag of shit but attractive." I nodded. Couldn't really disagree. But there are many lonely nights when I think about Dino Centro.

The phone broke my reverie. Marvin was downstairs. I buzzed him in and opened the door. Heard his hard clomp on the stairs. There wasn't going to be much subtlety in the room, unless I counted myself.

He nodded to Bailey Dao, but it wasn't a respectful nod. She offered him the bottle and he softened his look a bit. Took a healthy swig and offered his hand. They eyed each other, up and down, then shook. Marvin was wearing plaid pajama bottoms and a long leather jacket, no shirt. Hiking boots. He caught us looking, countered with, "A sweet disorder in the dress kindles in clothes a wantonness." Then he opened his coat to reveal a shoulder holster. Oh, God. "So are we doing this for the revolution or did somebody hire us? I figured I'd have to do some pro-bono work at first, make my reputation. If I solve this I'll have some cache with the police. Wally paid you something, didn't he?" This from Bailey, her eyes on Marvin.

"Yes, and he owes me some more, but I doubt I'll be able to collect. He wanted me to lead him to some people and I did. I'm expendable. I feel responsible for Terry, though. Don't you, Marvin?"

He opened his coat again. His PJs weren't very well secured. "I say we find Wally and shake him down for back wages. Then we put a bullet in his head."

"No way. I'll lose my new license." As she said this it occurred to me that I'd never seen a detective's license. "First we shake him down for your money, then we blow his operation wide open. Let Walgreen's take over the market. The publicity will get us lots of work. When I finish this sex change, I'll be the new Philip fucking Marlowe."

Bailey Dao was quite the careerist. I was worried about all that publicity. I didn't need the scrutiny. Could lead to an audit. Book scouts hate audits.

"Okay. I won't blow him away but I'll scare the shit out of him. Fucking capitalist."

"We'll put him behind bars and get rich in the process." Bailey Dao killed the Tequila. I went into the kitchen and found some more.

28.

Grace to be born and live as variously as possible. Amazing Grace. Tatoos and perfume. The double fuck. The double fuck! Who said I can't question someone that I'm sleeping with. She practically climbs into your mouth when she kisses you. Cool and dry shall come the results of inquiry. The double fuck! The place where the tattoos end on the upper arm, then the shoulder and the back of the neck, that Louise Brooks hairline.

They had stayed till about ten a.m., I'd slept till three, and now I was cleaning up and not quite calling Grace, putting it off they way you put off nibbling the last piece of icing on your plate. Too many questions could drive her away, or maybe not. Indecisiveness like that often gets me through dish doing and sweeping.

Cool and dry come the results of inquiry. I called Grace and left a message, juiced up the cell phone and took to the avenue. I was going to make my rounds, scout some books (I was running low in cash) and hopefully run into Bruce. I was pretty sure that there was more information in that rearranged head, if I could just break the code. I poked around Shakespeare and Co., then Moe's. No gaping holes in the shelves. Elliott and Laura were at the buying counter, tough hombres. It would be difficult to sell my wares, if I found some wares. I checked out the bestseller tables at Cody's to see what New York was foisting on us, then walked up Haste to the Tercel. Every good scouting day must start with espresso. I drove down to San Pablo, found a great parking place, and got in a rather long line at the Trieste. Scanned the room for Maser, White, or Jocko. No go. Not a book dealer in sight. All out hunting treasures, I suppose.

I found a table near the window and sat down with a second-hand sports page. I saw him crossing Dwight, weaving as usual, that huge knot on his forehead. Too tan from living outside. Head recently shaved. He crossed against the light, dodging cars. Surprisingly agile.

I waved, and he recognized me. He stopped at the

door. Had he been 86d? Probably just expected to be. The Trieste is a classy place. Not especially unfriendly, but some things go without saying. I got up and met him at the door.

"You've been looking for me."

"I was worried about you." He bowed his head. I felt that guilt that you feel on city streets, if you get out to the street, if you feel guilt. "Can I come in for coffee?" He didn't smell especially bad, but he looked pretty well worn. I wondered what the baristas would think.

"Sure, Bruce. I'll buy."

"You go up to the bar, okay?"

I ordered a double espresso. Not a second look from the barista. I felt good about the place. On second thought, I grabbed a pastry.

He downed the pastry in two chews, the coffee in a gulp.

"I have information, Clay."

"What's up?"

He was getting pretty wound up. He held the edge of the table and swayed. His face reddened. He worked his mouth without saying anything.

"Take it easy, Bruce." I put my hand on his shoulder.

"Can you spare some cash?"

I pulled out a ten. Detective work is expensive. He took it, looked at it with disdain.

"I need a hotel room and a shower. I got kicked out of my halfway house, I'm sleeping on cardboard."

"What do you know?"

"I know a lot."

"I'm not exactly rich right now." God. I was negotiating with a homeless person.

"I can tell you a lot if you take me to the pink motel on MacArthur and put me up for two nights." He nodded, too hard. "It will be worth it."

I'd already led a murderer to one victim. I wasn't going to do it again.

"Okay here's the deal. You tell me everything you can. Then you wait here. I'll go to the ATM and get you some cash. Then you take a cab to the Holiday Inn Express on University. Nobody will find you there."

He let out a guffaw. "I'm homeless. They won't let me in."

"I'll meet you there and check in. Then I'll hand off the key. You stay there 'till I come get you."

"Like a secret agent!"

"Just like. Now, what do you want to tell me?"

"They beat up Larry pretty bad but I don't know why."

"Who?"

Long pause. This was going to be a puzzle. I looked into his eyes. I imagined for a second that I could see through to the back of his head. Big white chunks of ambiguity sandwiched between red sections of unimaginable pain. He was reliving the beating. "I was outside Bongo eating a falafel." He drifted back into his head for a full minute. "You know where Joji's lot is?"

"I live on that block."

"Oh, yeah. I forget things."

"It's ok, Bruce. Tell me more."

"I saw Larry's van, parked in the lot. That's illegal, Clay. Joji gets real mad if you park there. I thought I could maybe get something to smoke from Larry. Sometimes he gives me stuff. I heard them talking, so I hid behind Joji's shack. They were asking where Terry was. They were hitting Larry. It sounded terrible."

"Who were they?"

He screwed up his mouth, then he went kind of buggy-eyed. I waited. He was feeling the punches. "The guy was British." He spit the words out. Did he not like Brits? "The girl was pretty. I only saw her from the back, but she was pretty."

"What did the Brit look like?"

"He was big."

"When did all this happen?"

A blank look. Bruce had little sense of time. "It was at night."

I bought him a second coffee and crossed the street to an ATM.

29.

I took a snaky back route to University, parked the car blocks away, took a little walk, entered the back door of an art store, came out the front. No evidence that I was being followed. Found an alley, came out on University near the hotel.

I found the office and registered at the Holiday Inn. Paid two days in advance, cash. Gave them a phony license number. Went out to the sidewalk. Out of habit, or something, Bruce was spare changing pedestrians.

"I need a little something for dinner."

I gave him twenty dollars. "I'll call a pizza place and have them deliver. Pay them with this. Don't leave the room. Just take it easy."

"Will they beat me up?"

"Only if they find you. Stay put."

I took out my cell and called Extreme Pizza on Shattuck. Was Bruce a vegetarian? To be safe I ordered a medium with mushrooms and peppers and a couple of cans of coke.

If Grace is the woman who beat up Larry I'll die, I thought, then I caught myself. Detectives can't be sentimental. Can they? How would I know. I put in a call to her, one to Bailey, and one to Marvin. Nobody home, anywhere. I pointed the Tercel down University, took a right on San Pablo, then a right on Solano, up to the Tibetan place. No van, no Larry. Decided to scout some books till something broke.

I hit a couple of second-hand stores on Solano. Only a couple of things, but it felt good to be scouting. I was born to root around old books. All those words, all those sentences, some of them great. Even the bad ones are amusing. Especially the bad ones! Old pulp, self-published poetry, somebody's first novel.

Lots of words, lots of books but nothing I could sell. I gathered up some pocket books. I could trade them at Moe's, maybe sell the trade slip to Julia Vinograd or one of the café intellectuals at the Med. I'd have to start going farther afield to get books. More trips down to San Jose, even LA. Ugh. Have to sell more business books online. This isn't why I got into the book business.

I drove down to Telegraph, did the deed, and did in fact sell the trade slip to Julia for half value. She offered to sell me her latest book of poetry, but I already had a copy. "That Larry guy with the kooky van is looking for you. He's parked in the lot at Brennan's. Says he'll be there all day. Gore Vidal didn't kill JFK. Did he?"

I downed my pinkie lifter and went back out to the Tercel. Back down University to Fourth Street. I was getting tired of driving.

Brennan's has been on that spot for as long as anyone can remember. I've never been in an Irish bar with more square footage. It's Chinese owned, but there's always a token bartender, pasty skinned and often a redhead. There are sandwiches, carved hofbrau style from big scary roasts. Not many places like this left in California.

30.

I ordered an Irish Coffee. I was on a caffeine bender. The alcohol would help calm me a bit. I nodded to Barry Gifford who was at the other end of the bar talking to a man with slicked back hair. Sadly, I was beyond eavesdropping range. They were probably discussing a movie deal.

The bar was dark. As my eyes got used to the light, I realized that the scraggly looking guy in the far corner was Marvin. With Larry! Why hadn't I noticed their vans? I paid for my coffee and went back to join them.

"Cuba's not what it used to be, but you'll do okay. All my old friends are gone. Only people I see there now are Fidel and his flaky brother. All dead, or sellouts. Or both."

"Do you think the glitterati will find me there?"

"No reason to look, Larry. Besides, your biggest problem now is big Wally."

"You don't know what you're talking about. Roth's out to get me. He could get a visa."

"No chance. Fidel hates Roth."

"Can I take the van ?"

"Larry! Dig this, Cuba's an island. You can't drive there."

Larry slumped in his chair, stuck out his lower lip, then noticed me. Frowned. I put my hand on Marvin's shoulder. He turned and smiled. I noticed that he was still wearing a shoulder holster.

"Clay Blackburn, I beat you to your clue. What do you think of that. Beat out you and your G-girl. Or is it G-boy? Larry here is on the lamb. Seems he was privy to some info regarding Terry and Drugstore Wally. Going to spill the frijoles if we get him safe passage. Right?"

Larry nodded. "Don't try and hit me, Clay."

I wanted the info, but I couldn't afford to send a stool pigeon to Cuba. What was Marvin thinking?

"We need to get Larry to a safe place, so he can talk. Then we need to get him on a plane. Okay, Clay?" This from Marvin, with a wink and a nod. I decided to play along.

"Where are the vans?"

"Larry's is in a safe place, and mine is down at the marina. We were being followed."

"Me, too."

"Big black SUV."

"Yeah, I noticed it too," I lied.

"There were at least three in the parking lot," he nodded toward Gifford. "One belongs to them. Do you think they're in on it?"

Larry looked at us with contempt. "Barry isn't part of the conspiracy." Rolled his eyes.

We needed a new ride. I decided to call around. Maybe somebody could pick us up, or maybe a cab. Pulled out the cell. There was a message from Bailey. I'd turned it off at Moe's because the buyers hate it when you take calls at the counter. Forgot to turn it back on. I called her back and she picked up. I explained the situation. "Hold tight and I'll think of something."

And so we ordered a second round. The bar began to fill up, working class types and serious drunks. And the mayor. I noticed him at a table near the door, talking to John McBride. Despite the representation of Berkeley celebs, Brennan's seems far from Berkeley. I imagined myself in the Barbary Coast, circa 1919. That stale beer smell, people gnawing on turkey wings. Only thing missing was cigarette smoke. Marvin regaled us with his tales of not-so-old Havana, and of trips back with suitcases full of cigars and rum. I could feel the hot sun reflecting off an Edsel, could smell the gas fumes and the cigar smoke. What was I doing in the US?

God help me, my cell phone plays "London Calling." I'm sorry, Joe Strummer, wherever you are. I couldn't help myself. It played the tune for Bailey Dao, tranny detective.

"Two cars. The lead car is an old VW fastback. You guys get in and the second car will run interference. Wait five minutes and go out the front door. Got it?"

We downed our coffee and hit the sidewalk as the cars pulled up. The second was an old Econoline, flat black, similar to Marvin's. We piled into the fastback, Bailey at the wheel. This was no ordinary VW. We were dodging cars and running lights, down to the Marina, around and back up University, right on sixth street. I assume the van was blocking the black SUV, or causing a diversion, or something. Bailey slowed down and we took a joy ride around town, and finally ended up at the Holiday Inn Express.

"I had it rebuilt. Great little car," she explained as she tore through the parking lot. She made a sharp left into an alley and parked the car. Illegal, but harder to spot. She was wearing a powder blue business suit, set off by the yellow, hip-hoppy running shoes.

I knocked twice and Bruce cracked the door, then let us in.

"I'm sorry I ate all the pizza." He and Larry gave each other the once over twice.

"Don't worry about that. We're going to put our heads together and solve this mystery." I hoped. I looked around the room, realized that I was the closest one to sanity. A rare occasion. I began with Larry.

"Who beat you up? And why?"

"An English guy and a woman with short dark hair."

"What did they want?"

"Terry was a double. They said they'd kill me if I told. And they told me not to get near you. That you're good as dead. "

Bruce nodded, so hard that I absent-mindedly rubbed my neck. "Terry wasn't Terry. No, no. Terry was Terry but he was made to look like somebody else. I told you that, Clay. You owe me money."

"How do you know this stuff?"

Bruce went all buggy-eyed. "Larry's father owns the building! And he won't even give me any pot!" He gave Larry a look that could kill, if it wasn't so comically cockeyed. "Trust fund baby!"

I exchanged looks with Marvin, then with Bailey. We had ourselves a client.

"I don't usually offer to help out capitalists, but I'll make an exception for you."

"They won't kill me if I don't tell."

"Too many people know. Someone will squeal, and you'll get blamed. Then, they'll come after you. Besides, you're not supposed to be talking to Clay here. This conversation could get you killed. " Marvin was laying it on thick.

"What are you going to do about it?"

"We'll chase 'em outta Berkeley."

I didn't buy it but Larry did. Six hundred a day plus

expenses, split three ways. Wouldn't make us rich but it would pay the rent. Bailey smiled her noble savage smile, leaned back, and closed her eyes. Rewriting her resume.

"I'll be broke within a week."

Bruce rolled his eyes. He seemed to have some secret knowledge of Larry's bank account.

Marvin gave me the stink-eye. He was going for a two-week contract and he knew I was getting soft. I decided to stop him. "Okay, Larry, give us a week. After that we renegotiate."

31.

Time to call in a few favors. I called a friend in Inverness, a few miles from Point Reyes. Billy Loy. He had two cabins. He lived in one, on a little rise, and he rented the next door cabin to tourists. He had a shotgun and a redneck mentality. If anybody tried to trespass, or if his tourist-tenants got out of line, out came the gun. I offered to rent the cabin but he said no go. I could have it for free for a week. I explained that a nut and homeless person would be living there and offered to leave a deposit.

"I've been renting to lawyers and financial types all year. They're boring and they're slobs. I'll bet they don't treat their live-work spaces the way they treat my cabins. A couple of loonies will be a relief. Hope they smoke the pot!"

Bailey came up with a plan involving two cars, alternate routes, and a nice lunch at a winery, where we got some funny looks. Guess we looked pretty Berkeley. Not many homeless people among the vineyards. Or transsexuals in three-piece Efrem Zimbalist suits (Bailey's outfit of the day). Throw in a Neil Young look-alike and you have a great group. Larry, the craziest of the lot, looks like a stockbroker. I can fit in anywhere. At least until I start throwing Dr. Pepper cans.

Three nice bottles of pinot for four is a perfect amount if you're driving. Shortens the road without too much impairment. Bruce put on a good show, swirling, sniffing, and practically gargling. His conclusion: not as much fun as smoking crack, but okay if somebody else is paying. We toasted Larry.

We took the narrow roads to the cabin with that special deftness that a partially liquid lunch inspires. We learned that Larry had a great singing voice. He'd adapted some of John Updike's dreadful poems, singing them Gilbert and Sullivan style.

"I respect those guys, assassins that they are. And I don't just do the big boys. Listen to this!" He lowered his voice and his cadence became more bluesy. A few verses into the song I recognized a passage from the avant-garde classic, "The Bellhop's Tears Kept Flowing" by Stephen Rodefer. I was impressed.

"I was a language poet after the surrealists kicked me out. No, check that. It was after Ron Padgett cut me in Gem Spa. Wouldn't even say hello. Berrigan, Clark, Notley… minor leaguers, really. A few heists here and there. Although I hear that Dick Gallup was a

Soviet Agent. But that's hearsay. Not worth repainting the van. Did you know that Amiri Baraka used to rob banks? He's calmed down a bit."

And he went on like that for a long long time. Finally Marvin had the presence of mind to ask for another song. "Do you know anything by Basil Bunting?"

He sang a song about a bull, and we were at the cabin before we knew it. There was a great-smelling breeze coming up from Tomales Bay. I could almost taste the oysters. What a great hide-out. Did we really need to solve this case?

Billy Loy came down from his place and met us with the keys. He was carrying an Oakland A's carry-on bag. We entered the cabin, one big living room and attached kitchen, a couple of small bedrooms and a bathroom. Big windows looking out at the trees. Wood stove, lots of books. We smiled. Billy smiled.

He opened the bag. "Who needs guns?" I hate guns, have never used one. I've done all right with a brain and my fists. I decided to swallow my disapproval. Guns might be a good idea. We were, after all, fighting a drugstore chain.

"Glocks for all! Got 'em from this guy who runs a speed lab. They can't be traced. But please, be careful. Don't shoot up the place unless you have to. I get two-fifty a night in high season." He gave me a look. "We're even after this, Clay."

"Even. Thanks Billy."

32.

Bruce looked longingly at Marvin's Glock. We wouldn't let him have one. Larry grabbed a gun, saying, "I paid for this microphone!" We watched as he loaded the gun. He knew what he was doing. Straight as he looks, it doesn't take a heath-care professional to know he's crazy. His eyes rolled to the ceiling (and the floor). "Lock and load!"

Marvin showed me how to load my gun though I protested. I wouldn't use it. Well, just in case.

It was still light, and warm. Late summer breeze and the scent of a forest fire, but off in the distance. I took a walk down to the bay with Marvin. He brought out his pipe as we sat on the beach.

"Who do you trust, Clay?"

"Bailey's okay. We have a good history."

He made a face. "She's a bit much, but I trust her."

"Bruce would go through hell for us, but he's likely to say the wrong thing."

"Well, yeah, the nuts. We'll hide them as best we can…"

"Larry's the money source. We're obligated to protect him."

"My only obligation is to bring down capitalism." He took a nice long hit, let it out , then a hooting laugh.

"We also have to pay for stuff," I said, pointing to his pipe.

"Point well taken. We'll hit him up for a big advance. Case he gets killed. And do you trust your girlfriend?"

"She hasn't answered my calls. I have to believe she's one of Wally's goons." My heart sank. The zipless fuck that wasn't.

Marvin put away the pipe. He put his hand on my shoulder. We were facing east, and the sun was getting low behind us. It hit the water on the shallow bay, bounced around the trees, glanced off the cars down the road. There were browns and golds, but the dominant color was orange. I thought of how terrible orange is, and life.

33.

Marvin's eyes got wide, wide as they could considering his marijuana intake. "Oysters! Johnson's will be closed!"

We raced up the path to the cabin. Bailey was drinking a glass of wine on the porch. We got the keys to the fastback and took off down the coast. Johnson's Oyster Farm is a ramshackle clump of old houses, hugging the oyster beds. We made our way past the dogs and cats that congregate under the "No Dogs Allowed"sign. Four dozen small, unshucked. Then back in the car and down to town. Bread, salad makings, many bottles of white wine. A serious situation calls for a serious meal.

We sent Larry up to get Billy and we arranged dinner. Bruce grabbed the shucker and proceeded to shuck, fast. "I used to do this for a living in New Orleans." Our secret lives.

You know you're in for a good meal when a couple of bottles are gone before you sit down. I was tipsy before I touched an oyster. They were perfect, and when they are, they are the perfect food. The wine was cold and clean. We had Tabasco and limes, but mostly we downed the oysters naked, followed by several good gulps of Sauvignon Blanc.

When the oysters were gone, we picked at the salad and the bread. When you've been through a few bizarre event turns you learn how to enjoy those moments of relaxation. Things got quiet, and I knew we were in for some interesting after-dinner conversation. Billy Loy must have sensed it too. He jumped up, ran out the door, and came back with two bottles of absinthe plus paraphernalia and a big chunk of hashish.

For a second, I thought it was a bad idea. Shouldn't we have a guard? Weren't we being followed? I decided not to mention it. Marvin was a soldier of fortune and Bailey Dao was ex-FBI. If they were willing to chance it, so was I. I also worried that Larry or Bruce might not handle it well. But what the hell. They couldn't get any crazier than they already were.

I hadn't had the hash/absinthe combination in years. It was in Barcelona, backroom of a bar, a night that revived my bisexual interests, after a too-long hiatus.

"If someone's chasing you down the street with a knife, you just run. You don't turn around and shout 'give it up! I was a track star at Mineola Prep.' You go on your nerve. That's the best part of doing what we do. Something clicks and you just move. There's freedom in that. It's outside all the rules. A sweet moment of anarchy."

I'd missed the set-up to Marvin's speech, but it didn't matter. Everything was humming along.

"Yes! You're the thing you're doing, you're not yourself. Look hard enough at something and you forget that you're going to die." This from Bailey, then a dramatic nod from Marvin. They were bonding, the lawman and the train robber. Same skills, same attitude.

I didn't comment. I was a rookie compared to these two. A book scout/poet who dabbled in crime solving. I downed the rest of my drink, got up and wobbled out to the porch. I spread my arms and let the air sober me up a bit, not too much. There was a nice pile of dry wood at the far end of the porch. It took me at least three hours to pick up some wood. Looking across the porch at the dark and the trees, I was about half an inch from an epiphany. As I waited for it to come across the porch rail, I noticed movement in the trees. I stood straight, listened hard, tried to focus. But my focus didn't last and there was no more sound. My epiphany disappeared, or was lost on me, like Kerouac's satori in Paris.

I marched inside and built a wood fire. Quite an accomplishment, considering my level of inebriation. I heard murmurs, then everyone moved toward the stove. Nobody said much then.

After a time that I can't measure, I decided to get up and go to the bedroom. Billy had put out sleeping bags and, I guess, gone back to his place. Everyone except Bailey was passed out in the bags, next to the fire. I tried one bedroom. Empty. I fell into a bottom bunk and passed out.

34.

Half-awake, the air smelled good. Too good. Perfume? For a second I didn't know where I was. Not the Chandler Apartments, I was facing the wrong way. Rome. Yes, Rome. The small bed. No, not Rome, the air smelled too good. Boulder.

That unmistakable, Tallulah-esque voice. "Just lie there. I'll do everything." The bag slipped away from the bed and I saw her sitting next to me. She'd somehow snuck in and taken off her clothes. Skin so pale it glowed. I looked up at the window. Too small. "Don't ask questions yet." Waking up to a blow job trumps all questions.

I gave it up too quick then listened to the crickets. I could feel the questions out there, not quite in my brain, circling. Give me a few more seconds, I thought. She was on top of me, but the questions won. No double this morning.

"I pretty much walked right in. You're all passed out cold. Some detectives."

"We're poets first. You know, a life of sensation…"

"Could get you killed. I'm here to warn you."

"Aren't you with them?"

She spread her arms. "Do I look like a Spirit of '76 type?"

"You look feminine, marvelous and tough."

"Poets."

"Didn't you beat on poor Larry?"

"I convinced them to let him go. Told them he was harmless."

"Why do they listen to you?"

"I've been working for them."

"Are you working for them now?"

"Yes and no. I'm cashing their checks, but I'm on your side. That's why I'm here. They didn't follow me, but eventually they'll catch up with you. They made you a top priority. A bunch of security goons are driving up from Orange County. You need to move fast."

"Move where?"

"Um. I guess that's up to you." She got up and dressed, almost silently. Dumb bad pop songs played in my brain. She slipped out through the living room, carrying her shoes.

35.

I turned on as many lights as I could find. There was much grumbling, but nobody went for their guns. Some detectives.

They sat, bleary-eyed, still drunk, and listened to my plan. Then they nodded. I have no idea if they understood. They must get it, I told myself. These are intelligent people.

I started the coffee. They understood that. We

had bought bagels, eggs, juice. I put together a quick breakfast. Always prepared, I brought out the Ramos Gin Fizz makings. Hair of the dog. I mixed, blended, tasted, doled out the drinks to the hangover sufferers. Just one. We had work to do.

I sent Bruce, drinks in hand, up to the big house to roust Billy. He returned with Billy and two empty glasses.

"That stuff's tasty! So, you want me to guard these two hombres while you cross the Orange Curtain into enemy territory."

"Look out, Anaheim. We'll take Mickey Mouse if we have to."

"I'll need to hire a coupla guys from the speed factory. They won't come cheap."

We all looked at Larry. "I'm not made of money. You'll bleed me dry."

"He's made of money. He owns the building." Bruce was getting riled.

"What building?" These nuts were getting on my nerves.

"The Chandler Apartments, Clay. He owns your building." He jumped up and pointed, vaguely, toward Berkeley. "And the UC Theatre building, and Black Oak Books and that Hawaiian bar on University."

I felt a little funny in the stomach. Was Larry my landlord?

I looked at Larry. He looked sheepish.

"I'll pay for the goons."

The fastback and Marvin's van were too noticeable, and the Tercel would have trouble with the grades.

We decided that a rental car would come under the expenses part of our contract. We called around and found a hotel near SFO where we could leave our car long-term when we took the rental. Bailey dropped us off at SFO to throw off our trackers. We walked around the airport, grabbed a hotel van and met Bailey in the parking lot. Walked to the rental car place.

They gave us a Buick. I didn't know they still made them. It was square as hell. Marvin liked that. "We're undercover." Put Neil Young and a transsexual giant in a midsize and you still have a circus. But I didn't say anything. I let him enjoy feeling mainstream.

"We're going down 101."

"C'mon, Marvin. Five's faster."

"A good soldier of fortune always spends his expense account. Besides, it'll be easier to throw them off our trail. They won't expect us to stay at the Miramar."

I looked at Bailey. She was a pro. Surely, an FBI agent wouldn't do something that silly.

"The pool there is great. Best to be well rested for a showdown. I could use a nice swim."

36.

Down past SFO, then beyond to San Jose, the industrial parks and the smog. Eyes open, looking for clones in black SUVs. Unfortunately, that describes at least half the population of central California. Perhaps they were all following the rented Buick. The air was warmer, then it was hot, we were in Steinbeck country, carpets of crops on either side.

We came to one of those Carl's or Denny's two-sided stops, got off at the Denny's. As we hit the off-ramp, I noticed a big yellow Hummer in front of the Carl's. Hard not to notice. There was no reason for me to suspect Spirit of '76, but I did. A real hunch! Maybe I am a detective.

"Let's park at Denny's and sneak over to Carl's. Check out that Hummer."

Head shaking and eye rolling, then "Why not?"

We walked through the underpass and snuck behind the trash bins, trying to look inconspicuous. They stayed back and I looked in the window. It was French, Metcalf and Wally. I remembered the words of the nuts. Wally isn't Wally. Were they headed back to the Bay Area? Were they following us, staying a little ahead to throw us off?

"There's one Wally and one French, eating big messy burgers."

Marvin pulled out a switchblade. I remembered the knife. We each bought one in Mazatlan, then smuggled them through security for fun. "Those big tires slash just as easily small ones."

Again it was me, the guy who can pass. Just another white guy admiring the patriotic car. I walked around to the back tires, smiling with appreciation. What a machine! The sun was really hot. I wished I had a hat. I popped the blade when the coast looked clear. Those big tires are really thick, but vulnerable. I got the two on the passenger side and came around. Two tragically fat kids, boy and girl, waddled by drinking Cokes the size of their heads. Dad lagged behind, with an even bigger Coke. Big, pink and round. They passed by me, I got the front driver's side, just a little poke before I saw another family exit Carl's. Lost my nerve and retreated to the bins.

"Marvin went to Denny's for burgers. Guess we'll eat in the car." Bailey had donned an A's cap. I wondered where she'd gotten it. We walked back to Denny's and waited in the car. Then we were on the road, burgers and fries in a blue Buick. I love this country.

We were climbing the pass outside of Santa Barbara. The Buick was chugging along. I was driving. Marvin was sacked out in the back seat.

"Did you see that?"

"Another yellow Hummer."

"There are lots on the road now."

"Another portly guy with a beard. Just like your description."

"Bailey, are your eyes that good?"

"You can't be blind in the FBI."

Going in the opposite direction. Maybe we had them fooled. I thought about Larry and Bruce, back at the cabin. I hoped that Billy Loy's boys had Glocks galore.

37.

We were sweating the traffic jam at State Street. We'd agreed on open windows, no air-conditioning, and the hot air was beautiful, a real novelty for Bay Area types. We noticed another Hummer but couldn't make out the driver. Darkened windows. Maybe it was Arnold. I remembered the days when Santa Barbara had a bohemian enclave, before the rents went apeshit. Surfers, beach bums, people passing through. Good times, back then. Just rich people now.

Ah, the Miramar. Just down at the heels enough. There's nothing like room service by the pool at the Miramar hotel.

We rented a two-bedroom cabana by the train tracks. Thank you, Larry. We dumped our stuff and I let my mind wander over my favorite Miramar story: Warren Zevon was having a nervous breakdown. Writer's block, drug problems, fame problems, whatever. He was holed up in a cabana. His hero, Ross Macdonald, came to visit. Zevon confessed that writing was no longer fun. Macdonald raised one eyebrow, waited (I imagine) a couple of beats, said, "Fun?"

"Fun?" had become another part of my secret language, shared only with Marvin. At some point in our stay here, one of us would repeat the phrase. We were both waiting for the right time.

Bailey Dao undressed for the pool. Marvin and I wanted to watch, made no pretense. Bailey didn't throw us out. As I said, her breasts were still woman-like, though small. She could never get away with going topless at the pool. This wasn't the south of France. She has the most beautiful pair of shoulders I've ever seen. Quite masculine, helped along with steroids and hormones, I imagine. Her stomach and her legs also seemed masculine, or maybe in-between. Her hands were man-sized yet feminine. Her face wasn't male or female, it was Bailey Dao. Impossible to place.

Six foot six, wearing men's boxer briefs, searching in her small carry-on. She pulled out a one-piece bathing suit, bright red, and disappeared into the bathroom. Marvin exhaled, then me. I wondered why she had brought her bathing suit. Did she know we'd stop at a pool when we went up to Inverness.

"I thought we'd go to the beach at Point Reyes," anticipating my question, emerging from the bathroom, ready for the pool. She grabbed one of the hotel-issue towels, went outside. "Meet you at the deep end."

"Is she pre- or post-op? I couldn't quite see."

"I didn't notice a bulge in her underwear."

"You've slept with one, haven't you Clay?"

"He was a cross-dresser. Different thing altogether, I think."

"I used to think I was totally straight. I'd make an exception for Bailey."

"Let's not get our hopes up."

I changed into a pair of shorts that I kept in the car. Marvin pulled a pair of sweats out of his old gas mask bag. He opened up his switchblade and cut off the legs. Tried them on in front of the full-length mirror, nodding and strutting. He looked like shit, but in an in-your-face way.

I grabbed the cell phone and we went out to the pool. Bailey had already been in; she was dripping wet on the lounge chair, eyeing a room service menu.

I got comfortable and we ordered some drinks. Dialed the cabin. Bruce answered the phone. "Hummers are cool, Clay. I drove one down to the lighthouse. They are a durable vehicle. Sometimes I missed the road but it didn't matter."

"Let's go back to square one. You have a Hummer?"

Long, goofy laugh. "We do now. Want to speak to Billy?" He passed the phone. An old Dylan song was playing in the background. I couldn't quite place it.

"They came in like gangbusters and my boys Glocked 'em. I didn't want to have to kill them, but these speed freaks think fast. Hell, they do everything fast."

My mind was reeling. They must have fixed those tires pronto. "Are they dead?"

"Doornails." I heard hooting and laughing in the background.

"The bodies?"

"Iced 'em down and sent 'em back to Monte Rio. Folks are friendlier over there. Wrap 'em up and throw 'em in the woods. Or send 'em down river like Lincoln Logs."

"What about the Hummer?"

"Got a buyer who won't talk much. Don't worry, Clay. I know about this stuff. But first I'm going to let Bruce drive it over to Bolinas. We're having dinner and drinks with Joanne Kyger. She'll get a hoot outta this."

"What did they look like?"

"Laurel and Hardy. Didn't give 'em time to say much. They missed, my guys didn't."

The Negronis came as I was relating the news to my poolmates.

"We may have them bamboozled. They'll send more people up north, and we'll slip into their territory."

"Bamboozled? Where'd you get that from?" Marvin had taken to teasing Bailey. Was he flirting?

"I hate to burst the bubble, but we don't know exactly where they are. Orange County's pretty big. Anaheim isn't, but still…"

Marvin gave me a poor Clay look. Babe in the woods. "I'm going to go into town and buy a laptop. Forgot to bring mine. A few e-mails, a few calls, a little research and we'll be knocking on Wally's door."

I remembered the Dylan song that they were playing in Inverness but I didn't bother to explain my chuckle. Marvin put out his hand and I handed him the keys to the Buick. He jumped up and went back to the cabana. He was back in a couple of minutes but he hadn't changed. He waved a credit card and went off to find a Best Buy. I wondered what the Santa Barbara sales crew would think when he plunked it down, said, "I'll take that one, no service contract."

Bailey waved a sleepy goodbye and fell into a nap. I walked down past the railroad tracks that run between the cabanas and the beach. I got a Coke from the machine and sat on the sand. Beyond the oil wells, the poisons were working their magic on the sunset. I watched the pinks, the greens, and the deep grays.

38.

"Don't worry about directions. We'll stay in one of those tacky motels near Disneyland. A rental car in a motel. Can't get more anonymous than that. And I have a contact. Worked with him in Angola, way back when. He's pissed off at the Wally bunch. Seems they cheated him out of his health care. It's stupid to get cheapskate with a soldier of fortune."

We were getting ready to go to one of the little Mexican places south of town. I could taste the Pacifico. Marvin was set up with the laptop, taking advantage of the wi-fi. He had a phone in his ear and he was leaning back with his eyes closed, rocking a little. Our information guru.

"He'll meet us at the motel and clue us in to the security system. Once we get inside, we'll... What will we do, Clay?"

I didn't answer because I didn't know what to say. We decided to come up with something over dinner.

They city smelled like salt and money for a few miles, then it smelled like salt and frying tortillas. We found a small place a few steps from the ocean. There was a mix of off duty waiters, gardeners, and slumming Santa Barbarans.

Over plates of beans and rice, we came up with a plan. If we could blackmail Wally into leaving us alone, especially Larry, we'd done our job. Discussing this, we realized that we were in a David vs. Goliath situation. We had to make him believe that killing us would be too much trouble. But first we had to find him.

Once satisfied that our plan wasn't too goofy, we ordered a full bottle of Campo Azul and lifted a few. I noticed a change in Bailey's countenance. She was smiling more, responding to Marvin's rough jokes, just generally loosening up. A good thing, I thought. Soon we'd be storming capitalism together. We'd fair better as comrades.

We drove back to the Marimar with the windows down, probably weaving. The air was perfect, and as we passed the pool I caught a telepathic jolt. Marvin was thinking what I was thinking. Was Bailey? The lights were off, except those in the pool. They probably kept those on for effect, or possibly to keep drunks and sleepwalkers from falling in. I took off my shirt and struggled with my pants. Had to sit on a lounge chair to finish stripping. That Campo Azul is strong stuff. Marvin did the same. Bailey stayed standing. She threw off her clothes in what seemed like a single motion.

We didn't want to splash too much. Wanted to have a good swim before getting thrown out. I slipped in and pushed off, floated, I believed, in total silence. There was a tequila time warp, seconds or minutes, who cares. I was sitting on the step on the shallow side and I heard them giggling on the other side of the pool. Giggling, hard breathing, harder breathing. I wondered what was going on. I mean, I knew what was going on. I wondered about the mechanics.

39.

We were at Malibu. Everybody was jolly, if a bit hung over. Blasting, beautiful mid morning. Welcome to LA. "Oddly green haloes surround summer love, my skeleton has gone on vacation." This from Marvin, quoting my poem "frm zuma to venice." I was flattered, and Bailey, who had no idea those were my words, was charmed.

Way down the coast, the slow way to go but pleasant, Redondo Beach, San Pedro, Long Beach, lots of water on the passenger side. My passengers had their heads out the windows, smelling the air like golden retrievers.

I turned the Buick east when I had to, and a couple of traffic jams later we were over by Angel Stadium. We found a business suite place with a shopping mall façade and checked in. We were watching a Dodger game on the big screen TV when our contact arrived.

He was as white male and square jawed as a man could be. Must have been a steroid case. Nobody has that much time to workout. Was he a cartoon? He looked like that Russian guy in the Rocky movie. Didn't introduce himself.

"Wallys are due in three places in the greater LA area today. There's another Wally in a meeting in Charlotte, North Carolina but he's not your guy." A steady look toward Marvin, who looked steadily back. No blinking allowed at this level. "You owe me big time, Marvin."

"I thought you owed me."

"Not any more. Wally's guys aren't especially good, but there's lots of them. He's a safety in numbers employer. They find out, they'll swarm me like ants. Bastards."

"Okay, I owe you. You have my number. Which Wally is our Wally."

"He's at the complex on Katella. Staff meeting, mostly sales people. Two bodyguards, security at the doors, but spread pretty thin. Not expecting trouble. He's pretty confident when it comes to appearing in public. He's got his doubles, you know. And he likes to mingle with the people. "He unzipped the front pocket of his orange windbreaker. Pulled out a parking sticker. Stars and stripes, '76 Priority, in script, across old glory. Three badges and a piece of paper. Directions.

He left without a goodbye. We went over our plan. Larry's information, along with the address of the complex, would be emailed to various papers and websites. We hoped to add a few pictures when we got inside. Should be enough to get the thugs to back off, maybe stop the operation. Good for Bailey's resume, even if the stories never got written. Word would get around that we were ace detectives. What the hell, the book business is dead. Dao, Clark, Blackburn detective agency. Or maybe that should be alphabetical.

Marvin put up an ideological argument for gutting Wally like a trout. We shook our heads. At least one bullet in his midsection? For the people? Again we said no. We loaded our Glocks. Marvin caught my squeamish look. "One bullet is worth a thousand bulletins!" Out the door and into the Buick.

40.

We breezed through parking security, thanks to the sticker. Walked, as directed, around, rather than through the metal detector. Security's prerogative. Just one guard at our door. He saw our guns and gave up with a shrug. No health insurance?

I was to do the talking. Marvin was disqualified. Too much commie rhetoric. I'd beat Bailey at the coin toss. Nice dramatic entrance, guns drawn, a chair kicked over for effect.

"No guns, no phones!" But someone had tripped an alarm, or something. Two guards followed us in. Bailey turned, a beautiful swivel. The red streak in her hair was in front of her face, then it wasn't, flairing back with the pivot. She crouched, gunslinger style, steadied herself splut one down, a small woman with very short hair. Bailey continued her crouch, got off the second shot splut through the head of a young Asian guy with slicked back hair.

Small caliber guns make little holes in people, but the holes soon get bigger and the life force, or whatever you call it, seeps out pretty fast. They weren't dead before they hit the floor, but they soon would be.

"Jesus, you're fast." Marvin was in love.

We turned to the cowering execs.

Marvin's cell rang. His jaw dropped as he listened. He looked with disdain at the suits, who were in a bunch on the linoleum. "They pulled a switcheroo. Wrong fucking Wally. He's across the street. He'll be in meeting there for the rest of the day.

We needed to get a look at the operation, find out where they turned people into doubles. Needed pictures of operating rooms. Wanted to scare a couple of doctors, too. But mostly we needed to get to Wally.

Marvin addressed the phony Wally. "We're terrorists. If you finger us you will die. There are thousands of us, pouring over the borders."

"Anything you say. I'm just a double. This is just a training session. Don't hurt us. We're not who we are."

We marched out, flashing our badges. "There's been a shooting. Don't go in there. Sit tight and wait for the authorities." Nobody seemed anxious to investigate.

We kept on marching and looking serious. Marvin took directions on the cell and we followed. Another generic building, low-slung with lots of chrome and tinted windows. Again we flashed our badges. So far we were getting away with murder.

We were in a hospital, or some kind of medical facility. We followed Marvin. We were passed in the hall by two Dick Cheneys! The better to avoid prosecution, I surmised. They smiled, gave a little wave. Bailey looked over my shoulder, caught my eye. This was a bigger operation than we'd thought. Government contracts. No wonder they had to kill Terry. Couldn't afford a loose cannon.

We walked into a room the size of a high school auditorium. It was about half-full of well-dressed familiar-looking people. There was a huge poster of Wally on one wall, cult-of-personality style. I recognized the Governor of Illinois, but I couldn't remember his name. Five Gwyneth Paltrows entered from a side door. One stepped up to Henry Kissinger, who kissed her hand.

"We need to lose ourselves in the crowd, for now." Marvin had a plan. God knows what it was. He pointed to the pocket that held the cell phone and gave a confident nod. Inside information. He pulled off his security badge and so did we. "You're a diplomat, and you're the daughter of the President of Quebecastan, a former Soviet satellite."

"And who are you?" Bailey was amused, not at all nervous.

"I'm Tom Waits."

"You look more like Neil Young." I, on the other hand, was sweating like a pig, feeling nauseous.

"With a haircut, I look like Lee Marvin."

"No you don't."

Wally entered the room. The security didn't look too tough. A couple of Sebastian Cabots and a couple of Metcalfs. No obvious artillery. Wally felt safe in his inner sanctum.

There were some small differences between this Wally and the first Wally that I'd met in the Suburbs. A little smaller, a little pudgier. When Wally made Wallys, he romanticized a bit. Who wouldn't?

He stepped briskly up to the mic, fronting his huge picture. This made him look smaller. The wizard, out from behind the curtain.

"Welcome graduates!" A nice round of applause. "I understand that you've been through a lot. Nips, tucks, voice lessons, new clothes, the like. Now you're at the end of the rainbow. A secure job, health-care, the American dream!" More applause. Two rows up, a Britney Spears clone was clapping and hopping, her perfect hair rising and falling, catching the light. "Soon you will be handed your orders, taken to your cars, and to your new posts. Some of you will be flying away. I am, however, disappointed to give you the sad news that we can no longer afford to fly you business class." The crowd didn't quite turn ugly, but the collective body language changed. There was a groan. "I know, my friends. Taxes, government regulations and the like have cut into profits. We all have to give a little."

I wondered how government regulations could cut into an illegal enterprise. Then, I wasn't wondering anymore. I noticed that Marvin had maneuvered himself to the edge of the stage. Bailey was at the other end. I understood. We were going to grab Wally as he left. I'd watch Wally, then break left or right, depending.

As he exited stage left, Bailey pulled out her security badge and followed him. I did the same, pushing a senator and a star first baseman in the process. I saw Marvin crossing the stage, bringing up the rear of Wally's entourage, Glock half drawn.

When I drew my gun, my pocket turned inside-out. Swift. I only vaguely remembered how to get the safety off.

We exited a side door. A parking lot was full of yellow Hummers and black SUVs. Must look pretty from the air, I thought. Checkerboard.

Bailey gave me a look that said, say something and I commenced to bulshitting. As a poet, I've trained for it my entire adult life. "These guys are imposters!"

"Of course they are, I pay them to be imposters. Who the fuck are you?"

"They're spies for the FBI."

"Ridiculous. I paid them off."

This wasn't going to be easy. "Okay, we're imposters. And we're going to shoot you with these really hip guns if you don't let us take you for a drive in one of these big dumb cars. We just want to talk a little business."

I eyed the Cabots and the Metcalfs. They were backing away, hands up. The health plans probably weren't that good. With little prodding, a Cabot handed over the keys to an Escalante.

I'd never been in one. Posh. Of course, I'd never buy one though, after all, even Mayakovsky once owned a Bugatti. The lure of great wheels!

Marvin drove. We got on the freeway and headed north toward LA. Bailey gave me that, "You do the talking look"and I launched into our plan.

"Okay, Wally, here's the deal. Terry gathered lots of info and he spilled the beans to a couple of Berkeley characters."

A roll of the eyes. "Berkeley. You guys don't deserve to be in America."

"Be that as it may, the beans, if I may extend the metaphor, have been removed from the scrambled brains of our Berkeley friends and re-spilled onto a bunch of emails. You don't have a license to change people into public figures. Bad publicity, Wally. Very bad. And you could go to prison. There must be laws involved."

I saw him fidget. That bean metaphor wouldn't make it in a poetry workshop, but Wally was a businessman. "Martha Stewart did fine after going to jail."

"Small potatoes. Are all your doctors licensed?"

More fidgeting. Maybe I had him. "In another couple of months, I'll have all that worked out. We just need to buy a few more politicians. After all, they use our services, too." A light came on in his eyes. The asshole thought he was at another seminar! "This is a great opportunity. I can let you in on the ground floor. Everybody needs a double. And it provides great jobs. When we work out the legal bugs, we'll have double centers in every Wally's Drugs and More. You can sit at the counter, order up a copy of yourself, fill in some forms, leave a video of yourself, come back in a week and pick yourself up."

I was surprised by his honesty. The beans were everywhere. "We could blow your operation before it gets started."

He was sweating. That rotary club façade was coming down. I watched his face grow mean. Willy Loman without the tragic side. Did we have him cornered?

"What do you want?"

"Stay out of Berkeley and leave us alone. That's all. We'll keep the evidence on file. Even if you buy your way into this scam, murder can get you into trouble. Homicide cops are harder to buy. One of them will want to make a name by frying your ass." I didn't know that, but it sounded good. "And no Wally's Drugs in the East Bay. San Francisco can fend for itself."

He sat for awhile looking out the window. We

passed through Long Beach, through Torrance. It was a beautiful LA day, low on the haze and not too hot. Marvin was having fun driving up the 405 in this rolling house. Bailey was silent in the passengers seat. As Torrance became southwest LA, I looked over at Wally. That blank, George Bush look was back on his face. Were the little wheels turning, or was he enjoying the ride?

Bailey turned in her seat. "Wally, here comes Compton. If you don't go our way with this, we're going to take this off-ramp and drop you off down there. And we may also shoot you in the leg. For fun."

A nice hoot from Marvin. He was definitely in love.

"Okay, okay. I hate Berkeley anyway. And Oakland. We'll open in Dublin and put you all out of business. You have your deal. It's not that important. Now take me back to Orange County. I don't like it here." Wally was beat. Could we trust him?

We got off in Compton and dropped him off. Gave him cab fair. CEOs never carry cash. Called a taxi. Left him on a corner in front of a beautiful stucco bungalow. If things got tough, he could always use his credit cards to buy the block.

41.

Back on the 405 going the other way, south to LAX, through much traffic to the long-term lot. Parked the tank and took the jitney to the Southwest terminal. I found the rental car desk and explained that, due to a terrible emergency, I had to leave the Buick in Orange County. The clerk, a little blonde guy with a movie star haircut, emoted sympathy then charged us a ridiculous pick-up charge. Expenses.

We got our tickets, smuggled the Glocks through security, bought an *LA Times* and settled in. I called Inverness to check on our little private asylum.

Bruce again. "I wrote a poem. Joanne says I'm a real poet. A poet in a Hummer!"

I mulled that one over for a few seconds. Had a vision of John Ashbery driving one. Mary Oliver? I don't think Al Young would drive one, even if he is California's poet laureate. Maybe Arnold should offer him one.

Billy Loy took the phone. "No visits from your friends. Somebody's coming to pick up the Hummer tonight. Larry wants the take, to cover expenses. I told him that half should go to me and the speed freaks. He can split the other half with Bruce. Sound fair?"

"Sounds fair to me. But you're the boss up there, Billy."

"Ten four."

42.

I was deep into a story about Lewis Macadam's attempts to save the LA River. Marvin and Bailey were sharing an order of fries from Burger King. For some reason (PI instincts?) we all looked up at the same time. Metcalf, or some reasonable facsimile. He was skulking behind some pay phones. Built to skulk!

"I'll pull a Sitting Bull and lead him to someplace quiet. Get ready to pull an ambush." We scanned the terminal. No French. There was a guy who looked a lot like Charleton Heston. A clone?

I once worked an airport security job at LAX. I checked IDs, looked at the x-ray, got bored. Most of the employees were ex-felons with doctored resumes. Their knowledge of weapons was firsthand, but they had little invested in enforcing the law. The airlines and the security companies didn't give a shit. They'd hire anybody that would work cheap. Probably still do. This was late seventies, early eighties. Drugs of choice: a mix of diet pills and pot. We had a great smoking spot. A little plot of lawn between American Airlines and the international terminal. There was even a tree, for shade. And it was near the least-used private restroom in the airport, for those who preferred the kind of drug that required a syringe.

I nonchalantly walked out the power doors and down the sidewalk. Just getting some air, no big deal. Metcalf followed at a safe distance. He was pretty good at being nondescript. Guess that's why they mass produced him. He was wearing a creased pair of light khakis and a blue knit shirt, the kind that have little alligators on the breast. I didn't get close enough for me to see the alligator.

I took a discreet look over my shoulder, got the lay of the land. No Hestons, no Cabots as far as I could see. The crowds thinned as I approached my secret spot.

I was approached on my left by a guy who looked like the sheriff in *In the Heat of the Night*. I was trying to think of the actor's name when he grabbed at me. The element of surprise almost worked, but not quite. I dodged right and caught him on the neck, just below his rather impressive left jowl. My second punch was to the solar plexus. Archie Moore, my old boxing teacher, would be proud. He didn't go down, but he was temporarily out of commission.

I walked briskly toward the bathroom, as planned. They would follow me in, corner me, and Bailey and Marvin would… shoot them in the back? I hoped not, but Marvin was unpredictable sometimes.

Incredible adrenalin rush as I stood, half crouched, in front of the trough. I always had to pee right before the fight. Nerves. Thought about taking advantage of the urinal, didn't have the time.

This Metcalf wasn't at all like the one we dangled out the window. Intense eyes, stretched face with no expression. Loosey-goosey stance, hands held just high enough. Wiry, probably quick.

"I've got back-up." He did that little neck move that fighters do when they loosen up. Shrugged his shoulders.

"Me too." I gave him my best stink-eye. Sonny

Liston, all the way. Where the fuck was Marvin?

I didn't notice the kind of bulge that a gun makes. Mine was back in my carry-on. Not that I'd use it. The real world melted away. I concentrated on the match-up. I was only a fair Golden Gloves amateur but I liked it. And it's why I'm a poet! Somebody told me about A. J. Leibling. After reading *The Sweet Science,* I turned to books and writing. This explains my boyish good looks. I got out before I collected too many scars.

He swung hard, missing with a couple of rights that were so clumsy that I thought they might be feints, designed to draw some counter reaction. He smiled, shrugged. I started to smile back. My lips were barely curved upward when he got me with a high left hook.

It wasn't a crashing knockdown, the kind that leaves you limp, like a wet hat, or jerky, like a new-caught fish. Most painful part was when my ass, then an elbow, hit the hard slippery tile.

It was a sit–down–and–think–it–over knockdown. To my surprise he let me do just that. Wasn't he sent to kill me? I looked around, got my bearings. Rod Steiger (I remembered his name. Thanks to the punch?) was still outside, presumably doubled over.

I got up. He danced around. Gave me a few seconds. I covered up and feinted, he bounced away. I was out-classed, I had to stall. In the stalls! I smiled at the joke in my head.

"Something funny, poet?"

"We're all a little crazy. Are they paying you full benefits?"

"Except for the business class thing."

"You guys need a union."

"Fuck that."

I caught him with a little jab that shouldn't have scored. Bad peripheral vision? The last guy I fought had nothing but peripheral vision. I moved left and caught his temple. Hard on the hand, but it made him flinch. I moved left, then right. He stared straight ahead. I caught some blows on the shoulder. They smarted but did no damage. Still no Marvin, no Bailey, no sheriff, no Heston.

There was a goofball fighter in LA, Windmill White. Almost won the light-heavyweight championship. He had a weird series of wind-ups, overhead punches, bolo-punches. One of his moves was to come around his opponent and tap him on the back. I danced around Metcalf. He turned his head, but he couldn't quite see me. I hit him with the hardest kidney punch I could muster.

"Foul!"

"This is a street fight, idiot." He was rolling around on the tiles. He hooked his right arm on the trough. I think he expected me to go to a neutral corner. I braced myself, got good balance, and kicked him in the head, hard. He slid back down. He wasn't completely out, but he wouldn't be going anywhere soon.

Bailey Dao entered the men's room as I was leaving. Sniffed and made a face.

"They smell bad, Bailey. Sure you want to be a man?"

"I'm my own sex, Clay. I have invented a sex. I'll explain it to you sometime. The guy with the chiseled face is dead. Drew on us, wouldn't drop his gun. Marvin dropped him. We couldn't pry the gun from his hand, so we threw him, and the gun, in a dumpster. Maybe he wanted it that way. That fat guy limped away. This part of the airport sure is deserted. Where's homeland security?"

"Probably watching a ballgame in the lounge. But we should move before the seventh inning stretch."

43.

We needed to make a statement. Needed to do something that would scare Wally off, or at least make him believe that we weren't worth the risk. We decided to hold onto the damning info a little longer. We'd take Metcalf back to Orange County and dump him at headquarters.

Metcalf was quite dazed. He took us to his black SUV and gave us the keys. Marvin insisted on driving. I got on the cell and somehow, convinced Southwest that my travel companions had taken sick with food poisoning and that I was taking them home. We were issued a voucher for another flight.

"I'm dumping the Econoline and getting one of these. They're no easier to drive, but feel the comfort!"

"Doesn't suit your lumpen style."

"Don't worry about that. We'll get Larry to paint a Che portrait across one side, Malcolm X on the other. A commie-mobile."

I was in the back seat. My Glock was in my lap,

but Metcalf wasn't going anywhere. I played with the gun. It was cool and light, with a sexy shape. Guns and SUVs, a slippery slope. Once you get on that streetcar named desire…

Marvin decided to change lanes. Every lane, all at once. Many honks. He sped up, did it again. I looked around for cops. He put on the radio and by some miracle found a station that was playing Coltrane. Turned it up loud. Nice ride!

We almost took flight as we rounded the off-ramp. Then down Katella to the headquarters. We circled the lot. There was a guard shack and a wooden gate at the exit. Marvin stepped on the gas, yelled, "Four wheel drive!" And we snapped the gate, but it had one of those don't back up tire things. Four blowouts. Bailey socked Marvin on the shoulder.

"You fucked up our ride, dickhead."

"It's okay. There's the Buick!"

The rental place hadn't picked it up. I'd palmed the keys. I'd have to call them and do some fast talking. Expenses.

We pulled up next to the Buick. Two rent-a-cops followed us, on foot. Guarding a parking lot was below Security '76. We pulled our guns and their hands went up.

"You guys have cell phones?" They stared at Bailey, nodded.

"Drop 'em, and your walkie-talkies and your guns."

"They won't give us guns."

"Okay. Take the rest of the day off.' And off they went.

We drove off, leaving Metcalf holding a note: "Dear Wally, we see your guys again and we blow the whistle."

44.

Dead of winter, Berkeley style. It was cold and clear early in the day, wind off the bay, no hint of smog. Dark and cloudy by five. I walked around the corner with a small bag of books. Nice looking stuff. Leather, Franklin Library. A Joyce, a Hemingway, *Tom Jones*, John Dos Passos, Willa Cather. Christmas stock.

The book thieves were swarming like vultures. New buyer at the Moe's counter. Slowdown John, Senior Scabarino, Bob Dark, Woofman, a tall guy in a slick suit who steals tech books. They mingled with the ex-cons, street folks, and sixties vets in front of Café Med. I decided to go over for a cup of coffee, just to check out the scene. I nodded to Julia Vinograd, ordered a pinky lifter and took a seat by the window. The light was bad, the room was drafty, the coffee so-so. Home sweet home. It started to rain, a little, just enough for the sidewalk party to move under the eaves.

An especially dodgy fellow stood outside the window and watched me drink my coffee. Acid victim, lost his mind in the revolution. Wild eyes, stringy hair. Showing some age now. How did he last this long?

Three months, no sign of the Wally squad. Also, sadly, no sign of Grace. Wally'd gotten himself in some trouble in Witchita. Bribed a couple of local officials. A tough DA brought one of his minions up on charges. No conviction. Marvin and I had talked about spilling the beans then but decided against it. Eventually the investigation would lead back to us and the case would be blown. A bisexual poet, an anarchist soldier of fortune, a transsexual ex–FBI agent. Bad witnesses.

And so we sat on the information. Larry and Bruce had started a beautiful friendship. They went to Italy for the winter, guests of Kathleen Fraser. Thanks to his start at Joanne Kyger's, Bruce had begun a career as a poet.

MBC Investigations did get some jobs, nothing involving CEOs, fistfights, or plastic surgery. Take some pictures, interview some suspects, drink martinis at Cesar. Expenses. A pretty good gig. I did as much scouting as I could, but the books were thin and prices were low. In the words of Jimmy Buffet, my occupational hazard's that my occupation's just now around. I'd been Amazon'd.

Skootch Leroux is a leggy book thief with a bit of a drug problem. Her look is disheveled, but not quite worse-for-wear. I watched her cross the street with a small stack of art books, covered in clear plastic. Her ass in tight black jeans, was a masterpiece, a miracle. A fuzzy, thrift store sweater didn't cover the tattoo on her lower back, a bird of some kind. Long black hair, moist from the sprinkle.

I decided to watch the fun. I covered my Franklins as best I could and crossed over to Moe's. Skootch was wiggling, dancing, leaning across the counter.

The fresh faced young buyer looked, almost leering, but not quite. Who could blame him? He smiled at her, then at me. He wasn't that green. The thieves would have to find another fence.

"I'm an artist, but I'm through with these. I'm sick of Klee and Kandinsky."

I was impressed that she pronounced Klee right. Berkeley has a well-educated criminal underground.

"Tired of the K's, I guess. Do you want cash or trade for these?"

"I wish I could take trade. I love books. But I need money for my brushes." Nice little flip of the hair.

Good thing I'm not a book buyer. I'd have given her all the money in the cash register.

"Sorry. We can't use these." He had round horn-rimmed glasses, kind of Harry Potter-ish. No wonder the thieves thought he was fresh meat. He looked too sweet for Telegraph.

45.

He gave me a good price for the Franklins, but not too good. We chatted for awhile and I went in for a browse. I wanted some new poetry. They have a great selection. I thought about Robert Lowell for a second, though I'm not a big fan. Read a few lines then put it back. I wasn't feeling East Coast neurotic. Almost fell asleep with quandariness. Lorca's too sad, and I was feeling a little sad. It occurred to me that I had been lonely since our big caper. This surprised me, because I'm not usually prone to loneliness. The pain of the passing of the last romance had snuck up on me, as winter came on.

I opted for a little Micah Ballard pamphlet, all gothic and spooky. The Keats of New Orleans.

Out into the night. Telegraph Avenue, empty and cold in that end of the year way, everything closed except one bookstore, one café, and Fred's Market. Wet copies of the *Express* lining the gutters, street folks hiding under anything that would stop the rain. My heart as desolate as a staircase. As the poet said.

Around the corner and up the stairs, feed the cat, put on some Townes Van Zandt. High, low and in between. A shot of the best whisky in the house, Oban. Settle in and read some poems.

The phone rang. The voice of Tallulah Bankhead, back from the dead. My pounding heart. Stay cool, Clay.

"It's fucking wet down here!" She was at the door. I buzzed her in and collected myself as she came up the stairs. I timed her entrance, opening the door before she could knock.

And it was her. Her-her. Grace & Grace. Grace twice. The short straight black hair, light light skin, sexiest mouth(s) I'd ever seen. I noticed that one was slightly taller. Which one was Grace?

"Move aside and let us in. We're quite wet." I recognized her as the real Grace. Well, the Grace I'd known.

But I was still confused. "Grace? Is it you?"

"What's left of me. This is Mina. We were discontinued."

"Fired?"

"Whatever. Somewhere there's a rich woman that looks like us. Guess she didn't pay up for her doubles. Or something."

What could I do? I went for the Oban. When life throws one a fish, you find a frying pan and chop up the herbs. I probably should have asked some questions. They could be working for Drugstore Wally.

But I didn't have questions. I had the answer to everything, the pot of gold at the end of the (double) rainbow. I poured the drinks and settled in for an incredible double fuck.

Fire on the Mountain

by Terry Bisson
Introduction by
Mumia Abu-Jamal
ISBN 978-1-60486-087-0
$15.95

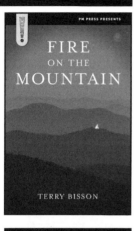

It's 1959 in socialist Virginia. The Deep South is an independent Black nation called Nova Africa. The second Mars expedition is about to touch down on the red planet. And a pregnant scientist is climbing the Blue Ridge in search of her great-great grandfather, a teenage slave who fought with John Brown and Harriet Tubman's guerrilla army. Long unavailable in the US, published in France as *Nova Africa*, *Fire on the Mountain* is the story of what might have happened if John Brown's raid on Harper's Ferry had succeeded—and the Civil War had been started not by the slave owners but the abolitionists.

ABOUT THE AUTHOR

Terry Bisson, who was for many years a Kentuckian living in New York City, is now a New Yorker living in California. In addition to science fiction, he has written biographies of Mumia Abu-Jamal and Nat Turner. He is also the host of a popular San Francisco reading series (SFinSF) and the Editor of PM's new Outspoken Authors pocketbook series.

from science to speculation and beyond—spectacular fiction offers the best stimulating writing for this world… and all the others.

Lonely Hearts Killer

ABOUT THE AUTHOR

Since his literary debut in 1997, Tomoyuki Hoshino has published twelve books on subjects ranging from "terrorism" to queer/trans community formations; from the exploitation of migrant workers to journalistic ethics; and from the Japanese emperor system to neoliberalism. He is well known in Japan for his nonfiction essays on politics, society, the arts, and sports.

What happens when a popular and young emperor suddenly dies, and the only person available to succeed him is his sister? How can people in an island country survive as climate change and martial law are eroding more and more opportunities for local sustainability and mutual aid? And what can be done to challenge the rise of a new authoritarian political leadership at a time when the general public is obsessed with fears related to personal and national "security"? These and other provocative questions provide the backdrop for this powerhouse novel about young adults embroiled in what appear to be more private matters—friendships, sex, a love suicide, and struggles to cope with grief and work.

LONELY HEARTS KILLER
TOMOYUKI HOSHINO

by Tomoyuki Hoshino
Translated by
Adrienne Carey Hurley
ISBN 978-1-60486-084-9
$15.95

Found In Translation is the finest way to experience the abundance of riches to be found outside of the English language.

About PM

PM Press was founded at the end of 2007 by a small collection of folks with decades of publishing, media, and organizing experience. PM co-founder Ramsey Kanaan started AK Press as a young teenager in Scotland almost 30 years ago and, together with his fellow PM Press co-conspirators, has published and distributed hundreds of books, pamphlets, CDs, and DVDs. Members of PM have founded enduring book fairs, spearheaded victorious tenant organizing campaigns, and worked closely with bookstores, academic conferences, and even rock bands to deliver political and challenging ideas to all walks of life. We're old enough to know what we're doing and young enough to know what's at stake.

We seek to create radical and stimulating fiction and non-fiction books, pamphlets, t-shirts, visual and audio materials to entertain, educate and inspire you. We aim to distribute these through every available channel with every available technology - whether that means you are seeing anarchist classics at our bookfair stalls; reading our latest vegan cookbook at the café; downloading geeky fiction e-books; or digging new music and timely videos from our website.

PM Press is always on the lookout for talented and skilled volunteers, artists, activists and writers to work with. If you have a great idea for a project or can contribute in some way, please get in touch.

PM Press
PO Box 23912
Oakland CA 94623
510-658-3906
www.pmpress.org

Friends of PM

These are indisputably momentous times—the financial system is melting down globally and the Empire is stumbling. Now more than ever there is a vital need for radical ideas.

In the year since its founding—and on a mere shoe-string—PM Press has risen to the formidable challenge of publishing and distributing knowledge and enter-tainment for the struggles ahead. We have published an impressive and stimulating array of literature, art, music, politics, and culture. Using every available medium, we've succeeded in connecting those hungry for ideas and information to those putting them into practice.

Friends of PM allows you to directly help impact, amplify, and revitalize the discourse and actions of rad-ical writers, filmmakers, and artists. It provides us with a stable foundation from which we can build upon our early successes and provides a much-needed subsidy for the materials that can't necessarily pay their own way.

It's a bargain for you too. For a minimum of $25 a month (we encourage more, needless to say), you'll get all the audio and video (over a dozen CDs and DVDs in our first year) or all of the print (also over a dozen in our first year). Or for $40 you get everything pub-lished in hard copy PLUS the ability to purchase any/all items you've missed at a 50% discount. And what could be better than the thrill of receiving a monthly package of cutting edge political theory, art, literature, ideas and practice delivered to your door?

Your card will be billed once a month, until you tell us to stop. Or until our efforts succeed in bringing the revolution around. Or the financial meltdown of Capital makes plastic redundant. Whichever comes first.

For more information on the Friends of PM, and about sponsoring particular projects, please go to www.pmpress.org, or contact us at info@pmpress.org.

About the Author

Owen Hill is the author of *The Chandler Apartments*, *Loose Ends* and several poetry collections. He was awarded the Howard Moss Residency for poetry at Yaddo in 2005. He lives in Berkeley, California, where he works in a second-hand bookstore.